Death Dream

Sorina opened her eyes to darkness. She felt the weight on her legs, the shifting weight of a small body that moved restlessly back and forth.

She started to laugh as she realized that, once again, the cat had found its way to her bedroom, but the laughter froze in her throat.

This night, she had locked the bedroom door. There was no way the cat could have entered. And then she smelled the smoke. She leaped from the bed, grabbed the key and jammed it into the lock. Nothing happened.

With mounting horror, Sorina suddenly realized that the carnelian cat had awakened her to meet a flaming nightmare of death. . . .

The Carnelian Cat

Birthstone Gothic #8

Jean DeWeese

BALLANTINE BOOKS • NEW YORK

SBN 345-24566-0-095

First Printing: August, 1975

Printed in the United States of America

BALLANTINE BOOKS
A Division of Random House, Inc.
201 East 50th Street, New York, N.Y.
Simultaneously published by
Ballantine Books, Ltd., Toronto, Canada

For Joetta, who, if she keeps at it, may be writing books of her own one of these years.

1

A faint tinge of reddish-purple twilight was still visible on the scattered clouds overhead as Sorina Stark maneuvered her battered station wagon through the iron gate and followed the tiny yellow sports car across the narrow bridge and up the long, curving gravel drive. In front of her, beyond the headlights, she could just make out the looming shadows of the chain of three houses that was strung along the broad loop made by the drive. The houses, as she knew from her visit earlier in the day, were about fifty yards apart and were connected to one another by enclosed, above-ground passages. The end houses in the chain—called, simply enough, according to Mrs. Hardy, West House and East House—were huge and square, two broad stories high, and made of a dark gray stone that Sorina had always associated with castles and small-town courthouses. Between them was a smaller house, also two stories high but less than half the size of either of the others. The servants' quarters, Mrs. Hardy had said, though it had not been used since East House had been vacated, a half century ago.

As Sorina's wagon rolled to an easy stop in front of West House, Mrs. Hardy was already out of her sports car and trotting hurriedly back toward it.

"I hope you don't mind if I rush through this," Mrs. Hardy said apologetically as Sorina climbed out and opened the back door of the wagon to get at her suitcases, "but I promised my husband that just this once . . ." She shrugged and peered into the back of the station wagon. "Here, let me get a couple of those suitcases for you."

"That's all right," Sorina said. "I understand. Anyway, Mr. Hunter showed me where everything was this afternoon. Just let me have the keys to everything, and I'll be all set."

"No, the least I can do—" The older woman stopped, half in and half out of the station wagon's back seat, and glanced at her watch in the faint glow from the dome light. "You're sure you'll be okay?" She looked back over her shoulder toward Sorina, standing a few feet away.

"I'll be fine. Don't worry about it," Sorina said, smiling. "I realize this was terribly short notice, and I appreciate all the rushing around you must have done to get it ready for me."

The older woman backed out of the car and stood facing Sorina for a moment. She was even shorter than Sorina's five-two, but probably topped her hundred and ten pounds by at least thirty. Her face, round where Sorina's was a soft oval, had concern written in every line.

"You're *sure* you don't mind?"

"I'm sure. You just go ahead. I need something to loosen up with anyway, after driving nearly four hundred miles today. Carrying a few suitcases will be just about right."

Mrs. Hardy glanced again at her watch, though she probably couldn't see it in the near darkness, and sighed.

"All right. But don't forget, if there's anything at all you need . . ."

"Don't worry, I'll get in touch with you. All I need right now are the keys."

"The keys, yes . . ." Mrs. Hardy dug through her purse for a second and came out with two key rings. "Here, this bunch is for the outside doors—front and back, garage, and the door to the connecting passageway. They're all marked. And don't forget, the front and back doors have those oddball locks; you need a key to get in and to get out. And these are for the rooms in the house. This one"—she picked out a key with a red tag attached—"is for your room, on the second floor. You know—"

"I know where it is. Mr. Hunter showed me everything this afternoon. Don't worry about me."

Mrs. Hardy hesitated a moment, then handed Sorina both rings of keys and returned to her car. As she pulled open the door and eased herself inside, she turned to Sorina for one last time, "Don't forget, anything at all . . ."

Sorina smiled and waved, and the car door swung shut. A moment later the engine roared into life, the headlights flared on, and the car rolled away down the long drive past the other two houses, across the second bridge, and out onto the road.

Sorina shivered momentarily in the cool autumn air and pulled the cardigan more tightly around her shoulders. In the distance, where the road turned and dipped and began its leisurely descent to the highway more than a mile away, the island of light that was the car retreated into the darkness.

She was alone.

She turned and looked up at the huge bulk of West House, and a feeling of unreality eased over her like a cloud. How long, she wondered, would it be until she could get used to the fact that for the next three months this monstrosity was to be both her home and her office? And, a perverse part of her mind added, how long would it be until she could look at it and not think: Three people were murdered here less than a year ago.

It was already too long, she told herself sharply! After all these years of forcing herself ahead, past all the obstacles she found in her path, this was no time to suddenly start going into useless fits of introspection and procrastination.

She shook her head, as if to clear such things out before they had a chance to take root, and hurried back to the station wagon and began unloading. In a few minutes she had her three suitcases, her ancient portable typewriter, the less ancient but equally battered TV set, and four boxes of books and various appliances stacked next to the front door.

Everything unloaded, she climbed back into the car. A garage with room for at least three cars butted up against the connecting passageway to the central house, and Sorina thought she might as well use it. It wasn't supposed to get particularly cold that night, but when a car gets to be ten years old, and it's been two years since the last tuneup, it can use all the help it can get.

No wonder Vern hadn't objected to her getting the car when they had separated, she thought irritably for the thousandth time in the last four years. The damned thing had been a wreck even then, although she hadn't realized it until a month later, on the first cold day of the semester. Already late for her first class, she had rushed from her room, dashed down the stairs and out the door, thrown her books onto the seat, and spent the next five minutes trying to start the car. In the end, she had walked—jogged most of the way, actually—and missed only about a half hour of her first class, but she had never trusted the rusting hulk since.

She winced as she opened the door and was greeted by the usual raucous squeaking of the hinges. Sticking the key into the ignition, she was pleasantly surprised when the engine caught immediately and even seemed to be hitting on all eight cylinders. Usually these short stops of only a few minutes did something mysterious and loathsome to the engine, causing it to refuse to do anything at all until she ground the battery nearly to death.

Just to be on the safe side, she let the engine idle for a minute before easing into gear. She wasn't taking any chances out here with the car. It was, since the phone had not yet been connected, her only means of getting in touch with anyone. Unlike Muncie, where she had spent the last four years, here there were no buses, and the five miles to Elston were a little too far for walking except in the direst of emergencies.

She switched on the lights, and the car, with only a slight grunking noise, moved down the drive toward the garage. As she approached the open door, she swung the car out toward the right, hoping that by swinging wide she could get inside without having to do any backing or maneuvering. The beast was only slightly smaller than a two-room apartment and not much lighter than a dump truck, so the lack of power steering made it about as maneuverable as a boulder.

As the lights swept across the grass—which from the looks of it hadn't been mowed for at least a month—and bounced off the trunks of the trees that were scattered throughout the grounds, something seemed to move at the periphery of her vision. Her eyes darted toward the spot for a moment, but the swath of light from the headlights had passed on by then, and she could see nothing.

It had been small, and there had been a brief glitter of reflected light, just a spot. An animal? It would have to be. Raccoons and the like showed up even in the city, so why shouldn't something have wandered in from the fields here?

The thought of backing the car around and aiming the headlights toward the spot crossed her mind, but only briefly. She continued the wide turn, and a moment later the car was inside the carage.

After a brief look around, she shut the lights and engine off, closed the garage door, and walked back along the drive toward the front door. Almost there, she stopped. Again, as it had when she had been in the car, something flickered in her peripheral vision. She turned toward the movement the instant it registered, but there was nothing there, only the nearly total darkness. The dozens of trees and occasional bushes were visible only as dark, amorphous outlines, and only the distinctive, forlorn shapes of the weeping willows were still recognizable.

An animal, she thought again, just an animal, and

she hurried toward the front door, where her suitcases and boxes lay waiting.

Inside, the house seemed even larger. The left wing, on both the first and second floors, was almost like a hotel—a single corridor running from the open, central staircase to the west end of the house, with at least a half dozen rooms opening off each corridor. Her own rooms—the "office" downstairs and bedroom upstairs—were near the ends of the corridors, and, as she dragged item after item up the long stairs, she wished she could have exchanged office for bedroom. Still, she thought, she couldn't complain. All in all, it had been a good, if hectic, day, despite the fact that it had started with a bleary-eyed seven-A.M. phone call.

"If you're really getting desperate," the voice had said as soon as Sorina had answered, "and you'd settle for something temporary, I may have just the thing for you."

"Jenny? Jenny Ward?"

"Jenny Hanson now, but that's close enough for this time of day. Now tell me, how do you feel about family histories?"

Sorina blinked a couple of times and wondered if the connection was bad. "Family histories?"

"That's what I said. How would you like to write one?"

"Me? You did say 'family histories,' didn't you?"

"Yes, family histories. Would you like to write one?"

"What family? And why?"

"The Howalds. I think I wrote you about them last year."

The name clicked in Sorina's mind. "Howalds . . . Isn't that the family that was murdered last year?"

"The same. So you see, you already know part of the history."

"What history? What the hell are you talking about?"

"The Howald family history, of course. I just found out that they left all their papers and correspondence to the Portman County Historical Society. Not only that—and this is where *you* come in—they provided some money to the Society to pay for sorting everything out and writing up a history."

"I don't really think—"

"Come on, Reenie, what have you got to lose? I'd take the job myself if they didn't have all those restrictions on it. And if I didn't already have a job."

"What restrictions?"

"No natives allowed, mostly, that's all. Guess they don't want any local prejudices to show up in the history. And if you don't take it, I'm going to keep going through my list of out-of-work friends until I find someone who *will* take it. And who will keep me informed at all times."

Sorina laughed in spite of herself. "So that's it," she said. "You just want an inside track on all the Howald dirty laundry."

"Who's denying it? They were the richest family in Portman County, maybe in this whole section of the state. Who wouldn't want a chance to prowl through all their correspondence for the last fifty or a hundred years?"

"Prowl, yes," Sorina said, "But read it *all*? For every juicy tidbit there'll be a thousand dry bones."

"Don't you think I know that? Just tell me the good ones. You can save all the dry stuff for the Society."

In the end, Sorina had agreed to make the two-hour drive to Elston, the county seat of Portman County in southern Indiana, and talk to someone at the Historical Society. From that point on things had happened fast, not because of any great urgency, but simply because it had worked out that way and because Sorina was rarely indecisive. Jerry Hunter, the balding president of the Historical Society, decided in short order that Sorina was just what they were looking for, and then, when he told her that the pay included rent-free use of part of the Howald home until the project was completed, she remembered that the rent on her own room back in

Muncie was due the next day. After a bit more discussion and a quick look at the Howald estate and the filing cabinets and boxes full of paper it contained, Sorina agreed to take the job and, if possible, to move in immediately. Hunter was unable to locate Norris Amers, the realtor who handled the land for the estate, but he found Joan Hardy, an associate of Amers'. By the time Sorina had driven back to Muncie, packed, told the landlady she was leaving, told the owner of the diner a few blocks from her room that he would need a new waitress that night, and then driven back to Elston, Mrs. Hardy had a bedroom and the kitchen in presentable condition, had the electricity turned on in at least West House, and had made arrangements to have the telephone reconnected in a couple of days.

All in all, she thought again as she unpacked the last of the suitcases, it had indeed been a fairly good day, certainly better than most in the past few years. A new town, a new job, a new—well, not a new life, but at least another step toward one.

She should, she supposed, let her parents know where she was, or at least her brother, John. But how? With the telephone not yet connected, she couldn't call them. But it wouldn't make a lot of difference, not really. There hadn't been that much contact between them in recent years, not since the divorce.

She frowned at the thought, and for a moment all the bitterness she had felt that day four years ago flooded back, bringing with it the countless memories she thought she had put behind her but that kept cropping up at all the wrong moments. Memories, such as that day in her freshman year at Indiana University, in Bloomington, more than eight years before, when she had first met Vern Malloy. And the night, sometime during the following summer, when they had agreed that they would marry and that Sorina would drop out of school—temporarily, of course—so she could help out with a full-time job until Vern graduated and got a job, at which time he would—of course—return the favor. And the afternoon, a few days later, when she had told her parents, and they had been so overjoyed and relieved—overjoyed because she was getting married, and relieved because they could now use the money they had spent most of their lives saving to help her younger brother, John, through school.

And the bitterest memory of all: That evening four years ago when Sorina had finally admitted to herself what she had been growing to suspect over the last two years—that Vern Malloy was interested only in Vern Malloy and that he had no intention, now that he had graduated, of fulfilling his part of the bargain.

"Come on, Sorina, what's so important about a degree? Besides, if you really want one, what's a little more time?"

And:

"After all, it's not as if I was asking you for something unreasonable. *Everyone* wants children! And if we have to wait another four years, until *you* finish school, too . . ."

She had left the next day, leaving behind not only her husband but his name as well. Her parents, as she had expected them to do, tried to talk her into going back to him. Only John had seemed to understand, but by then he had only another year to go in school himself, and he was planning to get married as soon as he graduated, so there was little he could do but offer his sympathy and show that he felt a little guilty about the whole affair.

But somehow Sorina had managed. With the help of a dozen part-time and summer jobs, she had made it through four years at the University in Muncie and had emerged with a B.A. in English and a minor in history. Unfortunately, the demand for such degrees did not come near to meeting the supply, so she had, during summer and early fall, kept on with the same type of jobs that had seen her through school. Sometime during those years the divorce papers had come through, and Sorina had noted with bitter amusement that Vern had gotten the divorce on grounds of desertion. The last she had heard, a year or so ago, he had remarried and was already on his way to achieving immortality through progeny.

And now? This job was at least a start. It wasn't perfect by any means, but it was by far the closest she had come to what she wanted. It could prove to be quite interesting, given half a chance, and when you counted in the free rent, the pay wasn't really that bad. If it lasted the three months that Hunter had promised, she would be able to put away a few hundred dollars, at least enough to see her through another few months of job hunting.

When she had finished unpacking and had everything either hung up in the huge walk-in closet or laid out in the large, mirror-topped bureau, she realized that she had neglected to pick up any food. Not that she couldn't stand to skip a late-evening snack just this once—or even an entire meal—she thought as she caught a sideways glance of her reflection in the bureau mirror. She was barely five-two, and her face, a broad oval with full cheeks and lips, always looked a bit on the heavy side, no matter how light she really was. But now . . .

Experimentally, she hooked her thumbs inside the waist band of her slacks. Tighter, much tighter than they had been a few months before. And her sweater felt a bit snug, too. Well, she thought, it's only to be expected. Now that she had been doing nothing but holding down a job for forty to fifty hours a week instead of working maybe thirty hours a week and then spending sixty hours a week on class work, it was bound to happen.

From somewhere came a harsh, buzzing sound, and, startled, Sorina looked around the room. It came again, and she realized now that it was coming from the hall. At the same time, she remembered what Hunter had told her about the doorbell that afternoon—that on the second floor it was a loud buzzer, installed to make sure the sound reached all the rooms. On the first floor there were the more conventional chimes.

She hurried down the hall and then down the broad, open staircase to the front door. Peering through one of the narrow, curtained windows next to the door was Jenny Hanson. Sorina threw open the door.

Jenny, four inches taller and four years younger, plunged inside and threw her arms around Sorina in a short, vigorous hug.

"You got the job, then," she said, standing back and looking at Sorina. "And of course you moved in immediately."

Sorina laughed. "Why not? My room rent was due tomorrow."

"Well, how do you like it so far?" Jenny looked around the hall animatedly. "No ghosts or anything like that?"

"I like it fine so far, but then I haven't done anything but move in. And no ghosts, either, so far. Now how did you know I was here?"

"I didn't, not for sure, but I figured it was worth a drive out here to find out. Once you agreed to talk to someone at the Society, I assumed that you'd get the job. And that if I came out here this evening, there was a good chance that you'd give me a tour of the place."

Again Sorina laughed. "And I suppose you'd like a tour of the Howald papers, too."

Jenny shrugged. "Why not? As long as I'm here . . ." She looked around again, her eyes coming to a stop a little to Sorina's right, next to the staircase. "Incidentally, did they show you where it happened?"

"Where 'it' happened?"

"It, them, you know what I mean. The murders. It was right there."

She pointed toward a spot beside the staircase and started walking toward it. "Abel was out here," she said, "near the foot of the stairs, and Clarice and the boy were both back here, half under the staircase."

She looked more closely at the thick, light-colored

rug that covered the floor. "They said they couldn't get the stains completely out of the rug, but it looks like they must have. Unless this is a new rug."

Sorina grimaced slightly, wondering if Jenny would ever outgrow her seemingly morbid fascination for murder. During the two years they had roomed together at school, a week had rarely gone by that Jenny hadn't unearthed another true crime or disaster book.

"Thanks a lot," Sorina said. "What are you doing, just making sure I *do* see a ghost tonight?"

Jenny looked back at Sorina and was silent for a moment.

"Sorry," she said, "I keep forgetting that that sort of thing isn't exactly your cup of tea."

"That's all right," Sorina assured her, "and I do appreciate your telling me about the job. Really. It sounds as if it could be pretty interesting. Now, you said you wanted a tour."

Sorina made a sweeping gesture with her arm. "This area you're standing in is the hall, I suppose. And there, on the right, through that big, arched door, is the main living room. You can tell because all those things under the sheets look like chairs and softs. And here . . ."

During the next half hour they poked into every room in West House, and Sorina had to admit that such exploring was fun, although they found nothing particularly unusual. Neither of them, however, had ever been through a house of this size before, and the number and size of the rooms, and the variety of furniture, though most of it was hidden under dust covers, all mixed together to make it seem more unusual than it probably really was. Jenny's only regret was that Sorina did not have keys to either of the other two houses in the complex.

They ended up in the room Sorina would be using for an office. It had apparently once been a den, although it now looked more like a storehouse. A couch and easy chair were along one wall, and opposite them a desk and swivel chair. Built-in bookshelves lined most of one wall, and in the middle of the floor were a half dozen filing cabinets and an equal number of cardboard packing boxes. As Hunter had explained, the cabinets had been moved here from Abel Howald's office not long after the murders, and the boxes of personal correspondence had been collected and moved here only a few days before, when the will's provision for donating them to the Historical Society had been revealed.

Jenny, of course, wanted to dig through them immediately, but Sorina convinced her that they would be there for several days and that there would be plenty more opportunities over the next three months. Privately Sorina was more than a little concerned about showing the papers to Jenny—or to anyone—without at least discussing it with Hunter or someone at the Society. Many of the papers were, after all, personal, and the Howalds deserved a certain consideration.

When Jenny left it was nearly ten. Sorina thought for a moment of glancing through some of the files herself, but rejected the idea almost immediately. Before she even looked at them she would go to the Elston library and read through the stories written about the Howalds when they had been murdered. There would be, at the very least, a short history of the family given in the articles, certainly enough to give her an overview, a skeleton to which she could attach the many pounds of paper flesh that lay in the filing cabinets and packing boxes.

And tonight . . .

Tonight, she thought with a sudden feeling of satisfaction, she would simply relax and feel happy and contented because, at last, the hardest part of her life was over. She was through school (at least until she had to return sometime in the next few years for an M.A.) and she had a job that promised to be interesting, even though it was only temporary. With a last look around the downstairs hall, she flicked off the lights and walked up the stairs. Half with amusement, half with annoyance she noticed that she carefully kept her eyes averted from the area immediately to the left of the stairs.

She would, she told herself, have to get over that kind of nonsense if she was going to spend the next three months here.

From somewhere there came a sound.

At first Sorina thought it came from the TV set, which she had almost forgotten was still turned on, now that the evening news was over, but it came again after she switched the set off.

Someone at the door? No, it wasn't a knocking sound. Besides, there was a more than adequate doorbell; no reason for anyone to knock. It was more like a faint scratching, like a shoe scraping across a bare floor. Or the claws of an animal . . .

Then she remembered the glittering spots of light she had seen outside the house as she had been putting the car away. Whatever the animal was, could it be scratching on the door? Or could it—or something like it—be inside the house somewhere?

Or could it possibly be rats?

She went to the hall door, stepped outside, and listened. But there was nothing, only silence.

A flashlight, she thought, I need a flashlight if I'm going to be out here in the country, away from the streetlights. If a fuse blew, she knew she would never find the fuse box, even though Hunter had showed her where it was that afternoon.

The sound came again, and this time she was sure it was something scratching, which was somewhat of a relief. At least it wasn't rats scrabbling through the walls. Rats were something she could definitely do without. There were few things she was openly afraid of, but rats were near the top of the list.

Moving more rapidly, Sorina walked down the hall to the staircase. She stopped at the head of the stairs and listened again, peering downward into the darkness. She touched the switch on the wall to her right, and the bottom of the stairway was flooded with light.

Slowly she walked down the steps, listening as she went. At the bottom the sound came again, louder this time, more distinct.

It came from the front door, she realized, and she moved toward it. She hesitated a second with her hand on the knob, then opened the door a crack. She looked out, down the steps, but there was nothing there.

She swung the door open farther, letting the light flow out onto the porch and dimly beyond, and, as she did, something moved in the shadows. It was small, an animal of some kind, just beyond the light-colored gravel of the drive, and it had moved rapidly, smoothly.

A cat? Could it have been a cat?

The scratching, now that she thought of it, did sound like a cat that one of her uncles had owned when they had lived on a farm in Ohio. It had been an outdoors cat, as opposed to the three indoors cats they also owned, but apparently it had never been happy with the designation, and every so often it would show up at the door and scratch for a few minutes. Just checking to see if there had been any change in policy, her uncle had always said.

But here? No one had lived here for nearly a year. Certainly if the Howalds had owned a cat, someone would have taken it. Or, if not, it certainly wouldn't have stayed around the house this long. It would have found another home, or, more likely, turned wild.

Frowning, she closed the door and turned back toward the stairs.

She was halfway to the second floor when she heard another sound. Not a scratching this time, but a faint, sharp thump, as if something had been knocked over in a distant part of the house.

Two animals? she wondered. Could one have gotten in while she had been bringing her luggage inside? She had, after all, left the front door wide open for several minutes, and anything could have wandered in. Two animals, one still outside, scratching to get the attention of the one on the inside, but retreating when, instead of the other animal, a human had come to the door?

Sorina swore briefly and softly under her breath, wishing again that she had a flashlight, something to shine around the yard, to probe the shadows. That was definitely going to be number one on her non-food shopping list the next morning. In the meantime . . .

She moved back down the stairs, this time turning to her left at the bottom, toward the east end of the house, the end connected to the garage and the passageway to the other buildings.

A wide, arched door led to a spacious living room, a dozen sheet-covered pieces of furniture giving it the look of an ornate mausoleum—a resemblance that Jenny had been quick to point out during their tour a couple of hours earlier. Paintings and prints, mostly still lifes and landscapes, decorated the walls, and in the middle of the opposite wall was a massive, open fireplace that went completely through the wall, so that it could be used from either side. To the left of the living room was a sliding door, partially open, that led to the music room, identifiable by the shadowy, sheet-shrouded form of a grand piano. Farther along on the left, behind another partially open sliding door, was the dining room.

For a long minute Sorina stood in the living room, listening, but there was now no sound, and she wondered if she could have imagined it. After all, this was her first night in a strange house, and, though she harbored no belief in the supernatural, she had to admit that having the spot on which the Howalds had been murdered pointed out to her had made her uneasy, no matter how hard she tried to tell herself that the feeling was foolish.

But no, simply being uneasy was not enough to make her imagine things. Something *had* made a noise.

She moved on through the living room and into the library beyond, and for a moment the sound was forgotten as she looked enviously at the floor-to-ceiling bookshelves that lined at least seventy-five percent of the walls. She shook her head, thinking: I'd better stay out of this room altogether, or I'll never be able to keep my mind on cataloguing papers and writing a history.

And she wouldn't find whatever had made the noise, either, not by standing and staring at the hundreds and hundreds of feet of bookshelves.

She hurried across the room to the far corner, where a plain wooden door stood almost hidden by the surrounding bookshelves. There was a bolt on it, unfastened, but no lock that she could see. She pushed the door open and peered through. A utilitarian stairway angled sharply down to the left, toward the rear of the house, and at the bottom was another door, leading, she assumed, to the garage. But there was nothing here, and no way an animal could have gotten in.

Closing the door and sliding the bolt home, she hurried back across the library, limiting herself to a quick glance at the fireplace that it shared with the adjacent living room. At the junction between the library and the living and dining rooms, she stopped and looked around again, wondering if there was any point in searching further. Even if she was sure that an animal *had* gotten into the house, the odds of finding it were small as long as it didn't want to be found. Even under normal circumstances, without the sheets draped over every major piece of furniture, there were hundreds of hiding places. An army of cats—or anything else that size—could be hidden all over the house and she would never know.

Another sound, and her head spun around sharply, her brownish, nearly shoulder-length hair swinging. Had it come from the dining room? Or from the kitchen beyond it?

Hesitating only an instant, she pushed the sliding door all the way open to let the light from the other rooms into the dining room. In the dimness and shadow, the huge table in the center of the room looked like a shroud-covered catafalque, and the dark, flowing drapes covering the window behind it completed the picture. Sorina shivered involuntarily as she peered into the shadows, listening to the silence.

The kitchen? On the right of the dining room was a large, swinging door, and Sorina crossed to it quickly. An animal couldn't have gotten in there, of course, but . . .

She paused and listened a moment before pushing the door partially open and stopping to listen again.

There was nothing, only silence.

She reached inside, fumbling on the wall next to the door, hoping to find the light switch, and all the time she listened, waited.

Suddenly, from behind her, there was a click, and a fraction of a second later lights flooded the room. She sucked in her breath with a gasp as she whirled around.

In front of the partially open door that led to the music room stood a man. He was tall, well over six feet, and thin. His hair was dark blond, and his beard, neatly trimmed but covering almost the entire lower half of his face, was a subdued red. His eyes were wide in puzzlement as he stared at her.

"Who the *hell*," he asked in a rumbling, bass voice, "are you?"

2

Sorina kept silent for a moment while she took another deep breath and regained control of herself. The man began to advance around the shrouded table toward her.

"Hold it!" she snapped, more authority in her voice than she felt. "Before you get any closer, who the hell are *you?*"

She began to edge sideways toward a low table next to the wall. Out of the corner of her eye she could see an ornamental candlestick, and her hand began to reach slowly in its direction.

"*Me?*" He stopped near the end of the table. His voice, though still deep, was a notch higher. "I own the damned place! Now who *are* you?"

She blinked and hesitated in her motion toward the candlestick.

"You own it? But I thought—"

"You thought it was empty and you could clean it out at your leisure?" He shook his head, glancing around. "Are you the only one?"

"The only *what?* Look, I don't know who you are, but I happen to work here! And if this is any sample of the working conditions, I don't think I'm going to last very long."

"Work here? What are you talking about? Nobody has—"

A look of sudden and disgusted comprehension creased his face, and a sigh escaped from his lips.

"The Historical Society! Is that it?"

"That's right. They hired me this afternoon."

The frown deepened. "Who? Hunter?"

"That's right. Just this afternoon."

He let his breath out in another sigh, and his eyes came to rest on her right hand, which was now only inches from the candlestick.

"You won't need that," he said. Again he shook his head, muttering something under his breath. "I'm Merrill Howald," he went on. "I don't suppose they told you about me."

"Abel's brother? They said you were in town, but they didn't say you were staying here."

"I'm not. I'm at the Fairview in Elston for the time being. I may—" He broke off, the deep frown returning. "Look, Miss Whoever-You-Are—"

"Sorina Stark," she supplied sharply.

"Miss Stark, then. I don't know how you— Look, are you from around here? Are you a buddy of Hunter's? Or what?"

Anger flared through her. His tone, full of patronizing irritation, was so damned much like Vern's had been every time they argued in those last months.

"No, I'm not from around here, and I'm not a 'buddy' of Hunter. I never heard of the man until this morning."

"Then how did you find out about the job? *They* only found out about the damn thing yesterday!"

"If you must know, a friend called me—Jenny Hanson. And if you're interested, you just missed her. She didn't say specifically how *she* heard about it. She's a teacher, so I assume she knows a few people in the Society. All right?"

"Yes, it's all right!" His voice indicated just the opposite. "But damn it, I—"

He broke off, shaking his head again. "Come on, let's go sit down someplace where everything isn't covered with a sheet. I suppose they've set up a couple of rooms for you?"

"Yes, they did. An office on the first floor and a bedroom on the second floor."

"Who did it? Amers?"

"Amers?" She shook her head. "What's an Amers?"

"Norris Amers. Among other things, he's the realtor who's been handling this place for the estate."

"Oh. No, Hunter couldn't reach him. Someone else, Mrs. Hardy, fixed things up."

"Oh, Joan. Yeah, she does most of Norris' work for him anyway, so why not this?" He motioned toward the other section of the house. "Now do you want to stand here within reach of your deadly candlestick all night, or do you want to go sit down? Your office perhaps?"

"It's fine with me, though I'm not sure what we have to discuss." She relinquished her position next to the candlestick, and they started back through the living room. "If you want to fire me, I suppose that's your privilege, although Hunter didn't say anything about approval being required."

"It isn't, it isn't," he said, his voice turning irritable again. "It's just— Well, damn it, it was so fast! I thought it would take weeks to find someone for this sort of thing."

"With jobs as scarce as they are today? Not likely. I don't mind admitting I snapped it up. I graduated over three months ago, and this is the first decent job I've had."

He glanced down at her as they passed the central stairway and neared the hallway leading to the office. "Just graduated?" He looked faintly skeptical.

"That's right, and if you think I look sort of old to have just graduated, you're right. I was delayed a few years."

He only nodded. His face, she noticed, was grim, and his mind seemed to be elsewhere as they walked. When they reached the office, he flipped on the light absently and sat down in the chair in front of the desk. His eyes seemed to be staring into the distance, and for a moment it was as if Sorina were not in the room. Then the eyes focused again, and he looked directly at her.

"You really *want* this job, then?" There was a tinge

of wonder in his voice, as if what he was asking was simply impossible for him to comprehend.

"If I didn't, I wouldn't have taken it, now would I?"

After a moment he smiled, as if in delayed reaction to the sarcasm in her voice.

"What if you were offered a better job? Before this one was finished?"

She shrugged. "I'd probably try to get it delayed. Or I might have to let it go by. I don't really know. It all depends on how much better the job would be."

She paused, eying him carefully. "What sort of job did you have in mind?"

"What sort of job did *you* have in mind?"

"A teacher, I suppose. That's where most English majors go. Although I wouldn't object to an interesting assignment on a magazine. Or a newspaper. I don't suppose the Howald holdings include anything like that?"

"As a matter of fact, they do. The *Elston Journal.* It's not big, but it's daily, at least."

"The local paper?"

"That's right. Or, if you don't like that prospect, I have a little influence with a couple of private schools in California."

She watched his face, trying to interpret his expression, but it was hard to do. The eyes showed little, and the rest of his features were masked by the short-cropped, reddish beard.

"You know," she said, after a brief silence, "I'm beginning to believe you're serious about this."

"I am," he said simply.

"But why? Don't you agree with your brother's will? Don't you want the family history written up?"

"I couldn't care less!" he snapped, irritation flaring up from somewhere.

"Then what—"

"This friend of yours," he interrupted, "the one you say called you about this. What did you say her name was?"

"Jenny Hanson. Used to be Jenny Ward. Do you know her?"

He shook his head. "I don't know a great many people in Portman County, not anymore. I haven't lived here that much in recent years. This Jenny Hanson—is she a friend of Amers'?"

"I have no idea. She didn't—"

"How did you happen to know her? Why would she have called you for something like this?"

"Mr. Howald," Sorina began, "if you don't have the authority to have me fired, I don't see what—"

"Just humor me," he snapped, and there was an icy hardness in his voice and his eyes.

She shrugged. "Very well. Jenny was a friend of mine at school. We had some of the same classes, even though she was a year ahead of me. And we had rooms in the same house for a while. And I'm not sure why she called me. Maybe she thought I needed a job."

"And did you?"

"I took it, didn't I?"

"Yes, you did," he said, some of the hardness going out of his tone, "with remarkable celerity, I might add."

"Why not? The work sounded interesting, and I had nothing to hold me back."

"And the name Amers doesn't mean anything to you?"

"No, it still doesn't mean anything to me," she said, a touch of irritation returning to her voice. "And it probably won't the next time you ask me, either. Should it?"

"I don't know. I thought possibly your friend had mentioned it to you."

"She didn't. And while we're on that subject, what does the name mean to *you?*"

He blinked. "Name? What name?"

"Amers, of course. Isn't that what we're talking about? What does it mean to you? Why are you so interested?"

The hardness came back into his eyes.

"No reason," he said, and Sorina could see that she would get no more from him on the subject.

"All right, Mr. Howald," Sorina said after a brief pause, "let's try to understand each other. As for me, there's nothing too complicated about it. A friend called me this morning to tell me about the possibility of a fairly interesting, if temporary, job here in Elston. I drove here this morning, talked to Hunter, decided the job really could be interesting, and took it. Even if it hadn't been that interesting, I might have taken it. I have just finished working my way through nearly four years of college, so I do not have a great deal of money saved, and the salary for this job is a lot better than anything I'd had so far. At the very least, I will be a few hundred dollars ahead when it is over. Therefore I took the job when it was offered, and I intend to keep it. Period. End of résumé."

She leaned back in the chair. "Now it's your turn, Mr. Howald. So far I've gotten nothing more from this conversation than a feeling that you don't want me here."

A reluctant smile, largely hidden by the reddish beard, spread across his face, and Sorina realized that, without the frown, he was actually rather attractive.

"Fair enough," he said finally, "and the first thing I suppose I should do is apologize."

"Not necessary," Sorina put in, "but welcome nonetheless. What I was rather hoping for, though, was an explanation."

The smile broadened into a grin, and he chuckled, a rumbling sound even deeper than his speaking voice.

"Yes, I imagine you would. Actually, it's no more complicated than your own story. Mostly my ill manners stem from surprise—the surprise of finding you, or anyone, here. Things have been moving a little fast. I've just been back in Elston for a few days, hoping to get the estate and the wills straightened out. You have no idea how complicated it can get when virtually all the members of a family are—" He paused, his face sobering. "When they all die at essentially the same time. And when no one knows in what sequence the deaths occurred. For example," he went on, sounding almost as if he were lecturing, "if Abel died last, then the bulk of the estate is divided among myself and a couple of cousins that I've never met. If Clarice was the last, however, it will mostly go to her family, although I will still receive a substantial sum."

He shrugged, glanced around the room. "But that is neither here nor there. I assume it will all be sorted out eventually. As I started to say, I've only been here a few days, and I learned of the grant to the Historical Society only two or three days ago. To be frank, I didn't pay much attention to it. It's a small sum, for one thing—only a few thousand dollars, I believe. The only reason I remembered it at all is that it's about the only item in the estate that isn't subject to dispute. The provision was in Abel's will, and it made no difference who died first."

He paused, lowered his head for a moment, and she could see him pulling in a deep breath before he continued. "The truth is, I had forgotten all about the grant this evening. I saw the light on when I drove by, and I sneaked in the back way to investigate."

"The back way?"

"Yes, in a manner of speaking. You saw how the three buildings are connected?"

She nodded. "Mr. Hunter told me the central building had been servants' quarters at one time."

"That's right. The whole thing was built by my—our—grandfather and his brother. One of them lived in West House, the other in East House. The servants lived in the smaller house in between. They could reach either house through the tunnels—or at least that's what I used to call them. In any event, I came in through the central house. The tunnel comes out in the kitchen. You startled the hell out of me, I don't mind saying. I thought you were a burglar at first."

"I don't suppose I can blame you. I have to admit, I did move in rather quickly. But it seemed like a good idea. For one thing, my rent where I was staying was due tomorrow, so—"

"Yes, well . . . I hope you'll forgive my initial reaction."

"Of course," she said, a little more readily than she had intended. "But one thing still puzzles me. Why were you quizzing me about Amers so much?"

For an instant the hardness returned to his eyes, but his reply was light.

"More spur-of-the-moment reaction, I'm afraid. I've never gotten along with Amers, and I thought he might have found out about the job and managed to steer one of his relatives into it."

"But why—"

"I told you it was a spur-of-the-moment reaction," he said, a touch of irritation returning to his voice. "I don't know what I thought, if anything."

Sorina decided against pursuing the question for the present. It would only make things worse, and she really didn't need the aggravation. Before she could think of something conciliatory to say, though, the doorbell rang.

Howald looked around sharply. "Are you expecting someone?"

She shook her head. "No. I have no idea who it could be. Unless Jenny forgot something . . ."

Merrill Howald followed several feet behind her as she left the room and walked down the hall. At the end of the hall he stopped short of the central area, standing just far enough out of the hall to give him a view of the front door. Sorina looked back at him, started to say something, but he motioned her to the door. She shrugged, puzzled, and opened the door.

"Miss Stark?"

The man standing in the door was, like Merrill Howald, somewhere in his thirties, but there the resemblance ended. He weighed about the same as Howald, but he was four or five inches shorter, and he was clean-shaven, the only concession to current styles being near-black sideburns that reached just below the bottoms of his ears. His face was square, the eyes deepset, although that impression might have been exaggerated by the shadows cast by the light mounted directly above the door. He wore a dark-blue suit and matching vest, the first vest Sorina recalled seeing in months. The last had belonged, she remembered, to a young history instructor the semester before last.

"Yes?" Sorina said. "What can I do for you?"

The man smiled, a boyish smile that seemed to take a half dozen years off his age.

"My name is Norris Amers," he said, holding out a hand, then letting it drop when Sorina did not take it. "Joan—Mrs. Hardy—said you had already arrived. I just thought I'd stop by to make sure you have everything you need."

A faint smile crossed Sorina's lips, and she glanced back toward the hallway. Howald was not visible, but she assumed he was still there.

"Won't you come in, Mr. Amers. Everything is fine. And a friend of yours has already dropped in to see me." She stepped back from the door to allow him in.

"A friend?" Amers' face reflected his puzzlement. "Mrs. Hardy, you mean?"

"No, she left some time ago." Sorina turned toward the hall. "Mr. Howald?" she said, raising her voice. "Are you still there?"

For a moment there was silence, and then Merrill Howald emerged from the hallway. He raised a hand in a half wave, half salute, but his eyes seemed grim.

"Norris, how are you?"

"Pretty well, Merrill. And you?"

"Fine, just fine."

There was a brief silence, then Amers spoke. "I heard that you were back in town. Plan on being here long?"

Howald shrugged. "It depends on how long it takes to get things settled."

Amers nodded. "Yes, the estate. That could be complicated, I suppose."

He turned toward Sorina. "And you, Miss Stark. I understand from Joan that you'll be here a few months."

"That's right. Three, theoretically."

"I see." He glanced at Howald, then back at Sorina. "Well, if you ever need anything, at any time, please call. I live just a half mile down the road, so I'll always be handy."

"Thank you," she said, "I may take you up on that—once the phone is installed."

"It's not in yet?" Amers' eyes rose slightly, and again he glanced toward Howald. "I'm sure we can do something to speed that up. Don't you think so, Merrill?" The boyish grin appeared fleetingly.

"Yes, I'm sure we could," Howald said flatly.

"Yes, I thought so. After all," Amers went on, turning partially toward Sorina, "most of the stock in the telephone company is owned by— Well, it *is* in the Howald name."

"True," Howald said. "I'm glad you reminded me. I've been away for a while, and— Well, things tend to slip my mind now and then."

He turned to Sorina. "I'll see what can be done tomorrow, if anything. Right now, though, I think I had best be going."

Amers watched the bearded man for a moment, then spoke. "Is that your car down by the middle house, Merrill?"

Howald frowned and stopped as he reached the door. "Yes, it is. Why do you ask?"

"Did someone come with you?"

"No," Howald snapped, "no one."

Amers nodded thoughtfully. "I thought I saw someone when I drove in, but I couldn't be sure."

"Saw someone? Where?"

"Down by your car. But I couldn't see anyone when I got there." Amers shrugged. "My imagination, I suppose."

"Yes," Howald said, his bass voice sharp, "no doubt it was your imagination. Imagination always did run in your family."

Amers said nothing, but his features stiffened and his eyes seemed to glaze for just a moment. Then an infinitestimal, icy smile flickered at the corners of his mouth.

"Or it could have been a convict, I suppose," Amers said softly.

Their eyes met, and for a moment it was as if Sorina did not exist, as if there were only the two of them, Howald and Amers, facing each other across a barrier that both knew would someday crumble.

"Yes," Howald said in a half whisper, "it could have been a convict."

He pulled in a deep breath and was silent for a moment before turning to Sorina again.

"Good evening, Miss Stark. I'll see what I can do about your phone. Sometime tomorrow, probably. And if you run into any problems with the papers or the history, please let me know."

"I will," Sorina said, a trifle uncertainly. "Thank you very much."

With an almost imperceptible nod toward Amers, Howald pushed through the door and slammed it shut behind himself.

Sorina turned to Amers after a moment. "What was all that about?"

Amers was silent, his eyes still on the door. Then, with a slight shake of his head, he turned back to Sorina.

"I'm sorry. I missed that. What did you say?"

"I asked you what that was all about? You said something about a convict, didn't you? Is there a prison in the area?"

Amers nodded, and he seemed fully recovered from whatever it was that had been disturbing him.

"A prison? Yes, the biggest in the state," he said, and Sorina thought she could detect a trace of pride in the tone. "Strictly speaking it's not a prison but a prison farm. The only trouble with it is, it's extremely easy to escape from."

He fell silent again, glancing toward the door as, from outside, there came the sound of a car starting and pulling away.

"They must not have told you at the Historical Society," he said as the sound of the car died away.

"Told me what?"

"About Merrill's brother."

"They told me that Abel Howald and his family had been killed a year ago, if that's what you mean."

"But they didn't tell you who killed them?"

"No," she said, irritation creeping back into her voice. It had been a long and tiring day, and Norris Amers was beginning to remind her of her ex-husband. How many more questions would she have to ask before he would give her a complete, direct answer. "Who *did* kill them?"

"An escaped convict. The prison farm is only four or five miles away."

Again he fell silent, and Sorina prodded, "What happened?"

"No one knows, not for sure. Abel and his wife and son were found shot to death the day after the escape. It was someone named Barlow. They found his prison clothes nearby a few days later, so they figure he must have taken some of Abel's clothes. They were about the same size, Abel and this Barlow."

Sorina was silent. With Amers' words the deaths became real to her for the first time. Until now, though she had known they had been murdered, though Jenny and Howald himself had referred to the deaths briefly, they had still seemed abstract. But now she could see the faceless bodies lying twisted and bloody by the staircase. Why, she wondered, had they chosen now to assert their reality? Was it because the words "shot to death" meant more to her than the general "murdered?" Or had it been his saying "Abel and his wife and son"?

"Why did he kill them?" she asked. "Was he holding them hostage?"

Amers shook his head. "No one knows. No one even knows why Barlow escaped in the first place. He had only a few more months to go on his sentence."

"What was he in for?"

"He'd been convicted of manslaughter—second degree, I think. A lot of people thought he should've been completely cleared, on the grounds of self-defense."

Sorina frowned. "He doesn't sound like a cold-blooded killer."

"No, he certainly doesn't. But something must have set him off—something that Abel or one of the others said. At least that's what everyone around here thinks." Amers shook his head. "That's one thing about killers, though, whether they're outright murderers or whatever—you can never be sure how their minds work. You can never tell what might trigger one of them."

"He was never caught?"

"They never found a trace of him. He simply vanished. The theory is that he took not only the clothes but some cash as well. Abel kept quite a bit around the house, and he never kept a record of it. As a result, no one knows for sure how much Barlow got. It could be nothing, or it could be a thousand dollars. Or more." He shrugged. "Enough cash makes it easy to get around inconspicuously."

"How did he escape in the first place?"

Amers laughed harshly. "He just walked away. It's easy enough to do. The prison farm is just that, a farm, with your average farm fences. No walls, no barriers except around the barracks, where the prisoners are kept at night. If a guard gets the least bit inattentive, a prisoner can just walk away. It's that simple. Or drive away. They even let some of the trustees go into Elston with a prison car."

Sorina looked surprised. "They certainly don't do that with the dangerous ones, do they?"

"Not normally, but who's to say who's dangerous and who's not? I remember once, when I was a kid, I saw one of them in Elston, no guard or anything. And *he* was a murderer!"

Sorina frowned, glancing toward the door once again, toward the darkness that lay beyond.

"I assume they increased security after the Howalds were killed."

Amers shook his head, a look of bitter amusement on his face.

"Not enough to notice. Oh, they tried for a while. Warden Crozier made a personal trip to see the governor, to ask for money for more guards. But nothing happened. Not enough money to go around, as usual."

"But don't the people around here worry about it?"

"They did for a while, but it's getting back to normal. The killings were a huge sensation for a week, and a major subject of conversation for a month, but . . ." He shrugged. "I suppose it's like living in California. Everyone says an earthquake is coming, but no one worries about it. Or like living in any large city. People are getting mugged and burglarized and murdered every day, but no one worries about it much. Unless it happens to them or their family."

"Yes, you're probably right, but still . . . Has anyone else ever escaped?"

"Sure, it happens all the time. Barlow is the only one who ever killed anyone, though—so far."

Despite herself, Sorina was suddenly smiling, almost laughing. "I must say, Mr. Amers, you have a way of making a person feel at ease."

His face lengthened. "I'm sorry. I didn't mean to frighten you, really."

"No, that's all right. I understand and I'm not frightened. Or at least I don't think I am. I'll let you know in a couple of days."

He nodded. "Yes. Well, I had better be going." He

moved to the door. "Don't forget, I'm only a half mile down the road, to the east. If there's anything you need . . ."

"Of course. I'll give you a call—when and if I get my phone."

As Amers left, Sorina stood in the door, watching the car pull away, down the long drive, across the narrow bridge, and onto the road, leaving the grounds in darkness again. Low in the sky to the southwest Sorina could see a faint glow. Elston? Probably. It seemed to be in about the right direction, and there was certainly nothing else in this area that would generate enough light to make even a faint glow on the low-hanging clouds that were moving in.

For another moment she stood there, her eyes roaming over the darkened yard, half expecting to see, once again, the glitter of a pair of eyes.

But there was nothing.

She glanced at her watch as she went back into the house and closed the door. Automatically she started to lock it, but then remembered that to lock or unlock it from the inside, she needed the key. And the key, along with all the others, was in her room upstairs. This could get old very rapidly, she thought.

Still, better safe than sorry, and she hurried up the stairs for the key.

Sometime during the night Sorina awakened. At first, the total lack of light puzzled her. There should have been at least a little light from the streetlamps outside.

And then she remembered, and some of the feeling of disorientation faded. She was in Portman County, a hundred miles from Muncie, and the nearest street lights were five miles away, in Elston.

But why was she awake? She sat up, propping herself on her elbows, looking first to the right and then to the left until she located the faint glow of her tiny alarm clock. She rolled closer to it, getting tangled in the covers as she did, then reached out and picked it up, holding it close to her face. With the luminous paint long since faded from the hour hand, she could only see that it was ten minutes past something.

She thought of turning the light on, but she couldn't remember just where the bedside lamp was located. Somewhere behind the clock, but . . .

But she didn't really want to know what time it was. What difference did it make? All she was going to do was go back to sleep.

Then she felt it—a faint, shifting pressure, something pressing down lightly on her feet.

And a sound, faint and distant.

For a moment Sorina was frozen, an icy chill biting into her back, and she stifled an impulse to scream. She twisted sharply, away from the bedside table, and, still propped up on her elbows, she squinted into the blackness.

Then she saw them. In the midst of the darkness that seemed to swirl around her like a living thing, she saw them: Three faint, reddish spots of light, even dimmer than the faded numerals on the clock dial.

Three dim, fuzzy spots of light, floating in the air only inches above the bed on which she lay.

3

Slowly, somehow keeping from screaming, Sorina reached toward the table next to the bed. Her fingers scrabbled along the surface of the table, past the clock, reaching, probing for the lamp.

Then her hand was touching it, her fingers sliding up the narrow column of the lamp's base toward the switch.

And still the dots of light were there, and as her fingers closed over the switch and turned it, she again felt the weight shifting, moving relentlessly on her legs.

The switch clicked, and light flooded over her, filling the room, dazzling her eyes. In the sudden brightness her eyes ached, and she squinted painfully.

The weight moved again—and was gone.

And finally her eyes were open, the pupils adjusted to the sudden change. There was nothing on the bed, no sound in the room other than her own breathing.

Sorina sat up straight and looked around. The bureau, with her miniature TV set still on it. The chairs, one with the book she had been reading before going to bed still lying open on the arm. The closet door slightly ajar. The door to the hall—

It sat on the floor, only inches from the door, staring solemnly up at her over its shoulder.

In an instant she relaxed, letting her breath out in a huge sigh that was mixed with relieved laughter.

A cat.

It was only a cat, its eyes gleaming in the dark.

The spots of light she had seen outside the house had been a cat after all, and somehow, during the times the door had been open, it had managed to slip into the house.

But there had been three spots of light, she thought, and for a moment, a chill again brushed at her spine. She looked more closely then, and the apprehension receded once again as she saw, half hidden by the long white fur at the cat's throat, something that glittered like a third eye as the animal moved.

A collar, with some kind of decoration, that was all. And that, of course, meant that the cat belonged to someone. But who? Amers lived a half mile away, he had said, and she didn't remember any other houses that were closer.

There was probably a name on the collar, though. She pushed the covers back and swung her feet out of bed and into the aging slippers on the floor. It was a little chilly, so she grabbed up the equally aged but fully functional terrycloth robe from the chair and slipped it on over her pajamas. At Vern's insistence, she had worn a nightgown most of the time they were married, but she had never really gotten used to it and had gone back to pajamas—which she considered more practical and warmer—shortly after the split.

"Hi there, cat," she said in a soft voice as she started to shuffle across the floor toward the animal. "Where'd you come from?" She leaned over and held out a hand toward it as she approached.

The cat stood up and turned toward her. Its fur was long, mostly white with some large patches of tan and dark orange. Certainly not a pedigreed animal, she thought, but there was something about it, something in the way the eyes looked up at her as if it was somehow trying to communicate with her. But most cats are like that, she thought, shaking her head slightly, at least when they want something to eat. And if this one had been in the house all evening with nothing to eat . . .

As the animal looked up at her, Sorina looked again at the thing around the cat's neck. It was not a simple collar, as she had at first thought. It looked expensive, made of something other than leather, something softer, richer looking. And in the front, where a tag would normally have been, was that reddish-orange—

Yes, reddish-orange, but what was it? She squinted as she leaned forward. A piece of colored glass? Plastic? It would have to be something like that, of course, but at this distance it looked very much like a gem of some kind, a reddish-orange, glittering gem.

Still speaking softly, Sorina reached toward the animal.

"Here, cat, let's see what that is around your—"

In a move that seemed fast even for a cat, it whirled about and darted through the door, leaving Sorina grasping only empty air.

"All right, if that's how it's going to be . . ." Sorina pushed the door open the rest of the way and walked out into the hall. The cat was nowhere in the dim light that fanned out into the hall. "Come on, cat, it's the middle of the night. No time for games."

She fumbled along the wall until she found the light switch, and as she flipped it on, she saw the cat at the head of the stairs at the end of the hall, sitting as if it had been waiting for hours.

"Okay, cat, you want out? I'll be happy to oblige. Just keep going to the door, all right?"

It was at the bottom of the stairs by the time Sorina reached the top, but instead of going toward the front door, it ducked around behind the stairs, toward the back of the house—and toward, Sorina told herself, uneasily, the spot where the Howalds had been murdered.

Then, disconcertingly, it was gone. When Sorina reached the bottom of the stairs, it was nowhere in sight, not waiting at the back door or anywhere else.

For a few minutes she looked through all the open rooms on the first floor, but found nothing. So much for that, she thought. She could look for a month and not find the animal if it didn't want to be found. Maybe she should just leave the door open a crack and go back to bed. But no, that was foolish. That was how it had gotten in in the first place. Instead of this one going out, another one would probably come in and join it. From what she remembered of the Ohio uncle's cats, they were incredibly contrary, always doing just the opposite of what you wanted or expected.

Besides, after Norris Amers' information about the prison farm's security system—or lack of one—she wasn't too anxious to leave any doors unlocked, let alone wide open.

No, the cat problem would just have to wait until morning. Maybe some food or catnip would lure it out into the open, or into some smaller room where she could close the door on it.

With a last look around the stairway and down the halls, Sorina switched off the lights and went back to bed.

The cat was nowhere in evidence in the morning, and Sorina wondered if it could have found its own way in and out—a special door, an open window somewhere.

But before she could start looking seriously for a cat, even a cat with such a distinctive collar, she was going to have to get something to eat, so the first project for the day was to go to a store to stock up on food. Since she was supposed to have kitchen privileges, there was no point in spending extra money to eat out all the time. With restaurant prices what they were, she would have used up what little money she had saved before she got her first check from the Society in a couple of weeks.

By ten o'clock she had finished her shopping and had enough food in the refrigerator and kitchen cabinets to last her for at least a week, and she was cleaning up the kitchen after a late breakfast. She also had a small, two-cell flashlight, just in case. She had still not seen the cat, but she put a small portion of cat food and some milk on the kitchen floor and propped the door open a few inches so the cat could get at the food.

If any of it disappeared, she would decide the animal was still in the house and start to look in earnest.

Then she was back in Elston, at the library, looking through the issues of the *Elston Journal* that had stories about the murders. Aside from a couple of pictures, they added little to what Norris Amers and Jenny had told her. They did, however, give the capsule history of the Howalds, just as she had expected.

Abel's grandfather, Leroy Howald, and a brother, Aaron, had come to Portman County in the late 1800s and, together with some unnamed partners, claimed and settled a great deal of land. They apparently did well, for they built the complex of houses that Sorina was staying in shortly before 1900. Leroy and his family lived in West House, Aaron and his family in East House.

From land, they branched out into other fields fairly early. They bought the *Elston Journal* in 1895 and started the Portman County Independent Telephone Company in 1902. By the mid-1920s, when Leroy and Aaron died within a year of each other, they owned a half dozen thriving businesses, from the local movie theater to a metal stamping plant. Leroy had been politically active and had served two terms in the U.S. House of Representatives and held a number of state and local offices, both elective and appointive. Aaron was never elected to anything, but as publisher and editor of the *Elston Journal,* he was considered a political power, at least on the county level and occasionally on the state level.

Their sons, Martin and Aaron, Jr., took over the businesses and the houses when they were both in their twenties. Aaron, Jr., however, sold his interest in everything to Martin almost immediately and left the state. Martin continued in the footsteps of his father in both the business and political arenas until his death in 1960, after which his older son, Abel, then in his late twenties, took over. Little was said of Martin's younger son, Merrill, except that he had gone to law school out of state and had visited Abel only occasionally in recent years. The fact that Aaron, Jr., who had died in 1950 in Florida, had three daughters was mentioned, but the daughters' whereabouts was not. These, Sorina imagined, must be the cousins that Merrill had mentioned the evening before.

And that was it. Not much, but at least it would give her a start. She would have a map, however sketchy, to guide her through the reams of paper that jammed the boxes and filing cabinets.

On the way back to the house, Sorina stopped at the Historical Society Museum, which occupied one corner of a large section of land that was owned by the adjacent cemetery. The main museum building was a squat, rectangular building of brown and gray brick that had once been the Elston City Hall. A recently painted sign identifying the building hung from a rough-hewn post just to one side of the gravel path that led from the small parking lot to the museum door. Beyond the museum, beyond a line of uneven hedges and some oak and willow trees, Sorina could see some of the taller headstones in the cemetery.

As she approached the building, she could see that the door was slightly ajar, and the murmur of voices and the clacking and shuffling of shoes on a bare wooden floor reached her ears. She pushed the door open and stepped inside. There were no lights, but the half dozen windows let in enough of the bright, afternoon sun to fully illuminate the interior. Glass-covered display cases lined one wall, while rough, plank tables jutted out from the others. All were filled or covered with ancient, yellowed ledgers, antique typewriters, and a hundred other implements that Sorina could not identify.

Eight or ten people, mostly middle-aged, the men all wearing jackets and ties, looked vaguely out of place in the turn-of-the-century surroundings. One woman, also middle-aged but less formal-looking than the others, was standing to one side. She wore dark slacks and a long-sleeved gray cardigan that could as easily have been a man's as a woman's. Her hair was short, almost a bob; once black, it was now liberally streaked with gray.

Sorina stood by the door a moment, and the woman looked toward her, smiling.

"Good afternoon. Is there anything special I can do for you?"

"Is Mr. Hunter around?"

"Not today. But maybe I can help you. I'm Barbara Strickland, the 'curator' I suppose you could call it if you wanted to sound impressive."

"Oh, Mrs. Strickland," Sorina said, recognition coming. "Mr. Hunter mentioned you yesterday. I'm Sorina Stark. I—"

The older woman's smile faded for a moment, then returned in a subdued form.

"Oh, yes, he was talking to you yesterday, wasn't he? About working with the Howald papers?"

"That's right. I took the job. In fact, I moved into the Howald house last night."

Mrs. Strickland nodded, the smile slipping again. "That's too bad," she said. "Really too bad."

"What?" Sorina frowned. "What do you mean?"

The woman shrugged. "Oh, well, I didn't have my hopes too high anyway, but still . . . Don't take it personally, Miss Stark. It's just—" She paused, shaking her head briefly. "It's just that I wish to hell you were a house mover instead of a researcher, or cataloguer, or whatever it is you're going to be doing."

"A house mover?"

A grudging smile began to find its way back onto Mrs. Strickland's lean, almost bony face.

"A depot mover, actually. It's the first Elston depot, from back in the late 1800s. It's going to be torn down next spring unless we can find someone to move it for us. The people who own the land are more than happy to let us have the building itself—as long as we get it off their land before they start building a shopping center on it next summer. And frankly, Miss Stark, that chunk of money we're having to pass on to you would just about cover the cost of moving that depot. So you see . . ." She shrugged.

"I didn't realize—" Sorina glanced toward the others in the room, but they didn't seem to be paying any attention to either herself or Mrs. Strickland. "You mean you were forced to hire me? Mr. Hunter didn't say anything about that."

"Not forced to hire *you*, specifically, but forced to hire *someone*. At least that's what Handley, the lawyer, told us. A certain amount of money in Abel Howald's will was set aside for the Portman County Historical Society, and at least fifty percent of it was to be used to sort through the Howald family papers, catalogue them, and put together 'a brief history' of the family."

"Fifty percent?"

"Yes, fifty percent. The other fifty we can use as we see fit—provided we use the first fifty for you. Or someone like you."

Mrs. Strickland shook her head again. "So we'll get *something* out of it. Maybe even get the depot moved with that other fifty percent. But I'd bet that moving and restoring the covered bridge will get most of it. Covered bridges are Jerry's—Mr. Hunter's—thing. And I have to admit, I'd hate to see that old Walnut Creek monster go. And it probably will attract more attention than the depot, but still . . . The thing that gripes me is that we have to hire *anyone*, let alone someone from outside the county, to work on the Howald papers."

"Yes, that out-of-the-county restriction struck me as a little odd," Sorina said. "Jenny mentioned it, but Mr. Hunter didn't explain anything about it yesterday."

Mrs. Strickland shrugged. "Not so much odd, I suppose, as just plain frustrating. It does make sense, of a sort. Abel—according to Handley, anyway—wanted to be absolutely sure the history would be objective. He was probably right, thinking that anyone from around here was likely to be prejudiced one way or the other, what with the Howalds being a sort of microcosmic version of the Kennedys. I can't help but be frustrated, though. There are dozens of people in the Society who would be glad to do all that work—sort the papers, catalogue them, write the history—for free. I mean, hell, who ever heard of anyone getting paid for writing a family history for a local historical society?"

"I wondered about that yesterday," Sorina admitted, "but Mr. Hunter intimated that if it turned out well, you might try to interest a commercial publisher in it. Or at least that you might try to sell a short version to some magazine or the Sunday supplements of newspapers."

Mrs. Strickland laughed, not quite derisively but certainly not with an overwhelming respect.

"Mr. Hunter," she said, "has a lot of ideas like that. He's a frustrated novelist at heart, I think. Very frustrated, and once you get around to the history itself, I'm sure he'll be looking over your shoulder quite a bit. Not that commercial publishing is impossible. Anything's possible, but it's not very likely, as far as I can see. I suppose he wanted you to play up the murder aspect of it?"

Sorina shook her head lightly. "As a matter of fact, he didn't. He barely mentioned it."

"Oh? Well, I'm sure he'll get around to it before long. Maybe he didn't want to say too much for fear of scaring you off. After all, part of the deal seems to be that whoever does the work—you, I guess—stays in West House."

"It's a good thing, too," Sorina said, smiling. "Have you seen the mass of paper they have? There's at least a half dozen file cabinets and twice that many storage boxes."

Mrs. Strickland nodded. "I saw them. The cabinets and boxes, that is. I never looked through any of them. Handley was keeping a pretty close eye on them, like he was afraid someone would steal a few reams. I imagine a lot are from Leroy's terms in Congress. Congressmen collect a lot of papers."

Sorina smiled agreement. "And they generally save every one of them. Really, though, I'm sorry if I'm taking money away from your other projects."

The older woman eyed her curiously for a moment. "But not sorry enough to . . ."

She left the sentence hanging, a faint grin pulling at the corners of her mouth.

Sorina's smile broadened. "No, not quite sorry enough to donate my salary back to the Society. Not by quite a bit. I've been on a bare-bones budget for too many years now to turn down good money. The job looks as if it could be interesting, but not *that* interesting."

"Don't worry about it. I'd do the same thing in your shoes, believe me. In fact, I wouldn't mind doing the job myself. Unless they've done a good censoring job, there have to be a few skeletons in all those paper closets. How's it going, by the way?"

"That's why I stopped by. I was going to tell Mr. Hunter that I moved into West House last night with no trouble. And that I had a visit from the only surviving Howald."

"Merrill? Yes, I saw him the other day, when the lawyer told us about the will."

"He thought I was a burglar at first," Sorina said. "He seemed very surprised that you had gotten someone for the job already."

"I can't say I blame him. I'm surprised, too. We were planning to put an ad in the classified sections of a few college-town papers—Lafayette, Bloomington, and those—but we hadn't gotten around to it yet. Jerry said you heard about it from Jenny Hanson."

"Yes, she called me yesterday morning. Got me out of bed with the news, in fact. And speaking of Jenny, that's another reason for my stopping by. Is there any reason why I shouldn't let her look through the papers? She asked me last night, but—"

Mrs. Strickland grinned. "I don't see why not. I wouldn't want to be responsible for her having a frustration breakdown. But I suppose you really should check with Merrill, just to be sure."

"Of course. I can see that he might object," she said, remembering his reaction the night before. "I'll be sure to check before I do anything. And right now I had better get moving. So far I haven't accomplished much, except to lay in some food and read the stories the *Journal* ran about the Howalds when they were killed." She reached out to shake hands.

"I'll tell Jerry you were in," the older woman said. "Incidentally, is the phone connected out there yet?"

"It hadn't been when I left, but Merrill Howald said he'd try to get it in today." She stopped, remembering more of the exchange of the night before. "By the way, is there something going on between him and Norris Amers? A feud or anything like that?"

Mrs. Strickland hesitated a moment. "Not that I know of," she said. "Why do you ask?"

"Just the way they acted last night. They seemed suspicious of each other. And before Amers got there, Merrill as much as said he didn't like Amers."

Again there was a slight hesitation before the older woman answered with a shrug.

"It could be, I suppose, although it can't be very serious. After all, Amers is listing all the Howald land—what there is left—through his office. There can't be much of a feud going on, or Merrill would switch to another realtor."

"You're probably right. It can't be much. But that reminds me of something else that happened last night. Do you know of anyone living near the Howald place who owns a large, long-haired, mostly white cat? It must belong to somebody, considering the fancy collar it has on."

"Cat? No, I can't imagine who it would belong to. Norris lives as close as anyone, but he only has a dog. And the Hennings, they're about the same distance to the west of you. They may have a cat or two, but I doubt that they'd have any with fancy collars. Or any collars at all."

"Hardly anyone would have a cat with a collar as fancy as this one. The beast acts at home, though, as if it knew the place. It got into the house last night, probably while I was bringing my stuff in, and later it showed up in my bedroom. I couldn't find it this morning, though, but it must still be there somewhere."

"Maybe it's just exploring. It could be a cat that someone just dumped off. A lot of people will dump cats on a country road just to get rid of them."

"I doubt it, not with a collar like this one has."

"Don't bet on it. People do strange things, believe me. And they're just as strange here in the country as they are in any city."

Sorina nodded. "Possible, I suppose. If it's still around, and if I can catch it, I'll put an ad in the paper. Or check the lost-and-found ads myself. Maybe someone will advertise for it. But that's for later. As I started to say a minute ago, before I sidetracked myself, I'd better be going. I'll let you or Mr. Hunter know how I'm getting along with the work. How often do you want a report? Every few days?"

"No need for reports. Just so you finish before the money runs out in three months. And let me know if you get finished ahead of time. There are always other things you could help out with."

Sorina laughed. "Something lighter than depot moving, I hope."

And before she could get sidetracked again, she turned and, with a last goodbye, left.

The cat had not put in an appearance by evening, and the food and milk were untouched. About midafternoon the phone had rung; it was Merrill Howald, telling her that the phone was now connected and what her number was.

"Any progress on your project to immortalize the

Howalds?" he asked, and Sorina thought she could detect an edge of sarcasm in his voice.

"A little," she said, and explained her morning's activities at the library. "I'm just starting on the files now," she concluded, "which reminds me of something. Do you mind if someone besides myself looks through some of the papers?"

The voice that replied a second later was hard, brittle. "As a matter of fact, I do, Miss Stark. I do."

"Very well," she said, her own voice sharp in response. "And thank you for getting the telephone connected."

Even before she finished speaking, she regretted the tone she had used. He was, of course, perfectly justified in being irritated at her request. Before she could say more, however, she heard the click as Howald terminated the connection. She lowered the receiver slowly and thought briefly of calling him back. But no, not now. Later, perhaps. She would be seeing him again, certainly, so there would be plenty of time.

Later in the afternoon, Norris Amers stopped by. "No particular reason," he said. "Just on my way home, and I was wondering if Merrill was able to deliver on his promise."

"The phone? Yes, he was. It was connected sometime this afternoon."

Amers shrugged. "I thought he could do it. All it takes around here is a little pull in the right places."

Sorina thought of asking Amers point-blank what it was that he had against Howald—and vice versa—but decided against it. If the antagonism between them was important to the proposed history, there would be some indication of it in the papers, and she would prefer to have at least a vague idea of what the conflict was before she was given the undoubtedly biased versions of Norris Amers and Merrill Howald.

As for the papers themselves, she discovered rather quickly that she would have very little organizing to do. Everything was neatly sorted and classified into folders with names, dates, and subjects penciled on them. The only problem was that, with the exception of the two file cabinets full of papers from Leroy Howald's four years in Congress, there was very little in the folders. The entire contents, except for the Congressional papers, could have been consolidated into a single file cabinet, two at most, and she wondered why she hadn't noticed this when Hunter had shown the folders to her the day before. But then he had just slid a few drawers open for a quick look, and the endless folders did, at first glance, seem impressive.

The Congressional papers, though, might make up for the rest, and Sorina decided that was the best place to start. She would ask Howald about the others the next time she talked to him.

By evening she was through only the first of the eight drawers, and she already had dozens of her three-by-five file cards filled with notes. There were copies of bills he had introduced, very few of which had been passed. There were hundreds of press clippings—more than half, she noticed, from the *Elston Journal*. And there were endless campaign records; personnel records of those who had worked for him, both in the campaigns and in Washington; and thousands of letters, to and from constituents and to and from officials, locally and in Washington.

Unfortunately, much of the material was written or scribbled by hand, and by evening her eyes were beginning to ache from the strain. As a result, she was rather glad when Jenny Hanson called and invited her to have dinner with her and her husband. The first thing Jenny wanted to know, of course, was when she could get a look at the Howald papers.

"It doesn't look as if you're going to," Sorina told her. "At least not until I'm finished and they're in the Society's files. But I don't think you're going to miss much," she hurried on in an effort to forestall Jenny's protest. "At least half of it is from the two terms that old Leroy Howald spent in Congress, back around the turn of the century, and believe me, it's not that exciting. He doesn't seem to have gotten involved in any really burning issues of the day. Or any scandals, for that matter."

"But the rest—"

"There isn't very much more," Sorina assured her. "There are several drawers of neatly labeled folders, but very little in them." She shook her head. "To tell the truth, this whole exercise with the papers is beginning to look futile unless I find a lot more in them than I expect to now."

"But Barbara said there were a half dozen file cabinets and boxes, all full."

"That's sort of true. Two of the cabinets are full of Leroy's Congressional papers, but the others contain mostly half-empty folders. It's a little strange, now that I think about it. You'd think that if Abel went to the trouble of making out a will donating all the family papers to someone, he'd have made sure the papers were pretty complete."

Jenny sighed. "I suspect you're just trying to make me feel better about not being allowed to browse, but . . ." She shrugged. "But that's no reason to break up a friendship. And I'm sure you'd let me know if you found anything *really* interesting . . ."

It was fairly late when Sorina returned to West House, and she briefly considered browsing through the library for a few minutes. She knew it was impractical at this hour, however. With a private library of that size, there was no such thing—for Sorina, at least—as browsing "for a few minutes." Once she started, she would be there for hours. Some evening, she thought, when she had more time.

In the end, she indulged in a little nostalgia, a rare luxury for her during the past few years, and watched part of an old mystery on the TV late show. It was one she remembered seeing in the theater more than fifteen years before, and while it didn't quite live up to her memories of it, it was still a pleasant way to simply relax.

It was almost over—one more break for commercials, she thought—when she heard the noise.

The cat again? She should have, she thought, put out some fresh milk and cat food after throwing away the batch she had set out that morning. But maybe the animal would be less elusive if it was still a little hungry.

She got up, leaving the TV set talking quietly to itself on the bureau, and walked to the hall. There was nothing there, nor, she discovered a minute later, on the stairway. She stood listening at the top of the stairs, unsure of whether she heard anything or not. There was a wind outside, not strong, but enough to rattle a loose window if it hit just right. And certainly in a house this large there had to be at least one loose window.

At the bottom of the stairs, to one side, there was a movement. She saw only a blur out of the corner of her eye, but she knew it had to be something small and light. The cat, of course. What else could it be? The doors were all locked, the windows closed . . .

She hesitated, then hurried back to her room, got the small flashlight from the bureau top, and returned to the stairs. Now there was no sound, no movement, nothing. There were only the muted, distorted voices and faint background music drifting down the hallway from her abandoned TV set.

She slowly started down the steps. About halfway down she again glimpsed a motion out of the corner of her eye. As she moved to the railing and looked down, a momentary dizziness swept over her, and Jenny's words from the night before came back to her.

And for just an instant, there among the shadows in the lower hall, she could see the bodies—Abel lying sprawled near the foot of the stairs; the boy, Mark, a few feet behind him; and Clarice, half under the stairs, crouched back, as if trying to squeeze out of sight . . .

And in that same instant, as she stood looking down,

looking back into the past, a feeling of terror and helplessness swept over her, and she could see herself crouched where Clarice Howald had been, her arms raised, half in supplication, half in a vain attempt to ward off the bullets she must have known were coming.

Then the feeling was gone, as quickly as it had come, and Sorina stood alone, leaning heavily on the railing.

The feeling was gone, but its effects remained. Her heart still beat at a frantic pace, and a tingle of fear still brushed at her spine.

And the image of Clarice Howald still hovered in the back of her mind, a ghostly presence, watching, waiting . . .

Sorina blinked, shaking her head sharply, and she wondered: What sort of nonsense *is* this? So someone was killed here—so what? It happened more than a year ago, and it happened to people that I didn't even know. People I have no connection with.

Again she shook her head and pushed herself away from the heavy, wooden railing. With a deliberate step she went the rest of the way down the stairs and, just to prove to herself that she could, she walked around the bottom of the staircase, past the supporting beams, and stood looking down at the spot beneath the stairs.

The spot where—

Sorina sucked in her breath sharply. The spot. It was impossible, of course, but there seemed to be a darker area in the carpet, as if—

As if a shadow hovered over it, a shadow that reached across nearly a year of time . . .

But it was a shadow, of course, a trick of the light here beneath the overhanging staircase, that was all. Steadying herself, feeling the annoyance at her own actions growing within her, she let the air out of her lungs in a sigh and leveled the flashlight at the spot.

And of course it vanished, just as she had known it would, just as all figments of the imagination vanish when you shine a bit of light on them.

Just as the movements she had seen—*thought* she had seen—had vanished when she had looked directly at them?

But no, that was different. That was something that, at another time, she had seen completely and squarely. And there was certainly nothing supernatural about a cat.

Or rather, nothing more supernatural about this cat than there was about any other cat. Why, it wasn't even black. Almost the opposite, in fact. A good fifty percent white, with three or four large orange-and-tan spots. It wasn't far from being a long-haired calico, and it would be hard to find a less "mysterious" cat than a calico, at least in appearance.

No, this was something real, something simple. And it was something she really should be doing something about. Something like finding it and checking the collar for identification.

Then, as if on cue, she heard it, an almost inaudible mewing sound that came from the direction of the dining room. Sorina grinned and started toward it.

She hurried through the huge living room and, using the flashlight to locate the switch, turned on the dining-room lights. She looked around quickly, through the door that led to the music room, but saw nothing. Then she ducked down, lifted the sheet that covered the dining table, and played the flashlight under it.

There was nothing.

Still, there were dozens of other places to look. But she would have to be methodical about it, While she had been peering under the table, the cat could easily have ducked out either of the doors. She would have to close them, isolate the rooms from each other, and search each one separately.

She was in the process of forcing the huge sliding door between the dining and living rooms shut when the mewing came again. Sorina looked around sharply.

Again it came, and she frowned in disbelief. From the kitchen? How could it have gotten in there? The door had been propped open while the food had been sitting on the floor, but it had been closed now for several hours. And certainly, even though the door had no latch, it was too heavy for a cat to push open.

She abandoned the sliding door and went to the swinging door to the kitchen. Quickly she eased it open and slid through, careful not to let anything slip past her. Again using the flashlight, she located the light switch and flicked it on.

The kitchen was empty. Everything—all the counters and cabinets, the stove, the refrigerator, the freezer—reached all the way to the floor, leaving no spaces along the walls that the animal could have hidden in. And there was nothing in the rest of the room that she could not see under, just a plain, formica-top table, a half dozen straight-back chairs, and a pair of large serving carts.

There were two doors in addition to the one through which she had entered. One, another swinging door, led to what amounted to a huge pantry. The other, a plain wooden door with a knob and lock, led to a curving set of stairs that connected to the passageway to the central house. At the bottom of the stairs was the door to the basement of West House.

If the cat were anywhere, it would have to be in the pantry. With its swinging door, it was the only place the animal could have gotten to.

Sorina pushed the door open and, as a bare, low-wattage bulb flared into half-hearted life, she looked quickly around. It took only a few seconds to see that this room, too, was empty. The shelves were bare except for a coating of dust. There was no furniture, unless you counted the stepladder that leaned against the far wall, and there were no hiding places that she could see.

Ridiculous! Sorina told herself. It *had* to be here. She had heard it through the kitchen door; she had come into the kitchen through the same door a few seconds later, and there was nowhere else it could have gotten to.

She shook her head, half irritated, half amused, and returned to the kitchen. For lack of anything better to do, she hunched down and looked more closely at the bases of the cabinets, just to be sure they were all solid and did indeed go all the way to the floor.

They were and they did.

The other door, the one to the passageway? Maybe it wasn't latched. Maybe, after bringing in her groceries this morning, she hadn't latched it firmly.

She went to the door and pushed at it.

A relieved laugh burst from her as it swung open easily and, in the dim light, she saw the cat halfway down the stairs. It sat, very catlike, staring up at her as if it were patiently waiting for her.

"All right, cat, enough is enough." Switching on the lights and tucking the flashlight into the waistband of her slacks, she carefully closed the door behind her and started down the steps.

With a soft, high-pitched mew, the cat stood up and darted down the rest of the steps.

Sorina sighed as she reached the bottom of the steps and saw the cat halfway to the other end of the passageway. As before, it was staring at her, waiting, showing no sign of fear or apprehension.

"Okay, cat, now I've got you," Sorina muttered to herself as she walked along the concrete floor of the passageway. As she approached, the cat trotted the rest of the way to the door at the far end and again sat waiting, staring first at Sorina, then at the closed door at the top of the short flight of stairs.

As Sorina approached, the cat simply continued to wait, as if impatient to be let through the door. She reached down and picked it up, and it did not resist. She held it out in front of her, looking at it and at the collar, particularly at the reddish-brown stone in the front.

She blinked, looked more closely. It *wasn't* plastic!

And it didn't look like glass, either. And the collar itself—she stroked it gently with her finger.

Velvet? Could the damned thing be *velvet?*

Who ever heard of a velvet cat collar?

"All right, cat, let's find out who you belong to, right now. If someone gave you a velvet collar, they certainly want you back, right?"

She sat down on the steps, took the cat in her lap, and started to search for the buckle on the collar. After a minute she decided there must not be any—unless it was hidden under the stone.

She slid the collar around carefully, until the stone was at the back. She whistled softly as she looked more closely at the stone and its mounting. For one thing, the stone, whatever it was, was definitely not glass. The deep, rust-red color was too rich, too pure for that.

And the cut— At first glance it appeared to be a long, slender oval, almost the shape of the pupil in the cat's eye, but as Sorina looked more closely she saw that what looked like a smooth curve was in reality a dozen or more perfectly flat, delicately cut facets.

The setting, either made of gold or a good imitation, was a solid-looking oval slightly larger than the stone itself.

Well, if it was a buckle, it was a well-disguised one, she thought, and began to probe beneath it, feeling for a catch of some kind.

She had only a moment to work, however. Almost the instant her fingers slipped under the gem, the cat yowled piercingly, and in a flurry of feet and tail it was on the floor and running. Sorina, startled into immobility by the sudden yowl and the explosion of activity, stared after it.

At least, she thought after a second, it didn't scratch, and she held up her hands to look at them more closely, just to be sure.

"All right, cat, if that's the way it's going to be . . ."

She stood up and walked down the passageway after

the animal, watching it disappear up the steps toward the kitchen door.

"You can just stay out here, if that's how you want it. You're not getting away until I find out who you belong to. I'll stick some cat food out here into your cell, and . . ."

Sorina's voice trailed off as she moved up the steps toward the kitchen door. First she frowned, and then, as she reached the top of the steps and looked back down, she swore under her breath.

It was impossible, but the steps were bare. The cat was nowhere in sight.

4

Wherever it had gotten to, the cat did not reappear that night, and when Sorina awakened in the morning, she was ready to believe she had dreamed the entire sequence. There had to be an explanation, of course, but she could not imagine what it was. Animals, even cats, could not simply disappear, and she vowed that the next time she got her hands on it, she would not let go.

The papers were, in their own way, equally frustrating, and a quick inspection of the neatly labeled folders revealed that there was even less in them than she had at first thought. By noon she had decided the best thing she could do was drive in to Elston and talk with either Hunter or Mrs. Strickland. And on the way she could stop at the Journal and check their lost-and-found ads for the cat. Certainly if someone had lost this one, there would be an ad for it. She might also, she thought, start a subscription to the paper. After all, if she was going to be here for a while, delving into local history, the least she could do was make an effort to keep up with local current events.

As it turned out, she could find neither Hunter nor Strickland, but she did run into Merrill Howald not far from the Journal office. He was in good spirits and seemed to have forgotten their brief conflict over letting Jenny look through the papers. He waved aside her attempted apology.

"Don't give it another thought," he said. "I snapped first and you snapped back, that's all. You took me by surprise, the same as you did the first time, when we mistook each other for burglars." He smiled behind the beard. "You seem to have a talent for catching me off guard, I have to admit."

She returned the smile. "Yes," she agreed, "I think it goes along with my talent for charging into things without thinking them through. If I'd stopped to look at it from your point of view, I probably would never have asked."

"It's quite all right, believe me. You *did* ask, which is more than some people might have done, and I appreciate it." He paused briefly, his face becoming serious. "But it really would be best if no one else was given access to the papers. Not quite yet, at least."

She agreed and was about to ask about the possibility of any of the papers being missing, when they reached the Journal. When he discovered she was planning to get a subscription, he insisted on taking care of it himself.

"I don't know yet if I own this place or not," he said as he held the door open for her, "but as long as I'm here I might as well act as if I do. Now, you want it for how long? Three months, wasn't it?"

"That's right, but—"

"And delivered to West House."

"Yes, but—"

"Fine. It's all settled, then. It's on the house."

"No, really, I couldn't."

"You can, and that's all there is to it. Let's just say I'm making amends for earlier behavior."

"All right," she said finally, "if you say so."

And to herself, as Merrill made the arrangements with a bespectacled teen-ager behind the counter, she added: Why not? I can certainly use any money I can save. And someone with a lot of money, who's willing to spend a little of it on me, should be a welcome change.

Not only that, she thought idly as she watched him, he was certainly attractive enough in other ways. Or perhaps intriguing was the word. Thin, but not, she realized as her eyes moved over him more slowly, excessively so. Just in good shape, that was all. The shoulders did broaden out quite a bit from the narrow hips, now that she thought about it. And the beard . . . She had never been especially attracted to men with beards, but neither had she been turned off by them. And this one, tinged red, neatly trimmed but masking his face almost entirely from high on his cheeks to below his chin, was at least a real, no-nonsense beard, not a tiny decoration like the one Vern had been sporting on the point of his chin the last time she had seen him.

The memory of her ex-husband, and the thought that she had had virtually no male companionship in the last four years, brought her rising mood back down. Money or not, intriguing or not, Merrill Howald was so far just an acquaintance, and it would be best to leave it that way—for the time being, at least. Get back into the swing of things gradually, at least as far as men are concerned. Don't jump in head first, like you do everything else—or let yourself get pulled in head first. That's what you did last time, she told herself firmly, and look where it got you.

Taking her eyes away from Merrill, she glanced around the office. A half dozen desks were arranged behind the waist-high counter, and a glass-windowed cubicle stood near the rear. To one side, a set of steep stairs led to an enclosed balcony, and from somewhere she could hear the jangling of a phone and the continual clatter of a teletype machine.

"Incidentally," she said when Merrill looked up from the counter, "do they have a copy of yesterday's *Journal* around here?"

"I'm sure they do." He turned toward the office and spoke to a balding, slightly paunchy man at a nearby desk. "Floyd? You still have yesterday's paper?"

"Sure, Mr. Howald," he said, pushing his chair back and coming forward to reach under the back of the counter. He pulled out a paper and dropped it on the counter.

"Thank you," Sorina said, spreading the paper out.

"Sure you wouldn't want a job here?" Merrill asked, his bass voice barely above a whisper so that no one else in the office could hear. "The offer is still open. Or maybe you'd like one of those other jobs I mentioned?"

She glanced toward him as she unfolded the paper, looking for the classified section.

"Ask me after I've finished the job I'm on now," she said.

He shrugged. "Just checking. What are you looking for?" he asked as he saw that she was running her finger rapidly down the columns of ads.

"Lost and Found," she said. "You do have one, don't you? Yes, here it is."

A puzzled frown crossed Merrill's forehead. "I didn't think you'd been here long enough to have lost anything."

"I haven't lost anything. I found something. Or was found *by* something. A cat. And it certainly isn't this one," she said, pointing at one of the ads. "It's a Siamese, and the one I found is most un-Siamese."

"You found a cat? Where?"

"As I said, it found me. It's in the house somewhere. At least I think it is." Sorina paused and looked up at him. "Are there any cat or dog doors in that house? Doors a cat could open by itself?"

He shook his head, his expression still puzzled. "Not that I know of. Unless Clarice added them. She was pretty much of a cat person, I understand."

"She owned a cat?"

"I think they had two or three," Merrill said, "but I understood that one of her sisters took them."

"Does the sister live around here?"

"I don't think so, but—" He turned toward the man who had gotten Sorina the paper a minute before. "Floyd, do you know where Clarice's sister lives? The one that took the cats? Remember, you were telling me about her at the funeral."

Floyd looked up. "Emma, you mean? I don't know, exactly. Somewhere in Illinois, I think. Why?"

Merrill turned back to Sorina. "I don't know. Why do we want to know?"

"If she's nearby, the cat might have strayed back, that's all."

Floyd shook his head. "Not likely. Unless she's moved, she and her husband live at least two hundred miles from here."

"It's possible, though," Merrill added. "I've read about cats that traveled great distances to get back home."

Sorina shook her head. "Not this one. It seems to be in perfect shape. Clean, well-groomed. It obviously hasn't been doing a lot of cross-country traveling lately. With hair as long as it has, it would be full of burrs and everything else, especially at this time of year."

Floyd seemed interested. "What sort of cat? What does it look like?"

"No special breed as far as I can tell. Medium size, mostly white, very long hair, some large patches of orange and tan. Looks as if it could be a long-haired calico if it tried. But the collar is what's really unusual. I'd swear it was velvet, and it has a gem of some kind in it. A large one, and it's either genuine or a very good imitation."

Now Merrill frowned, not an annoyed frown, but a skeptical one.

"What sort of gem?" he asked.

"I don't know. It was very clear, had a great deal of sparkle even in that dim light last night. And it was—well, rusty red is the best I can do to describe the color."

"What shape?"

"Oval. A rather slender oval, almost like the pupil in a cat's eye. And the setting, believe it or not, looked like gold."

Merrill's frown deepened. "Would you recognize the

stone—the type of stone, I mean—if you saw one like it?"

Sorina thought for a moment. "Possibly. I don't know a lot about gems, though, so I couldn't guarantee anything."

"That's good enough," Merrill said. "Look, why don't we get something to eat, and then I'll take you down to the library. Maybe we can find some pictures of it."

"All right," Sorina agreed, "but before we go anywhere, I'd like to put an ad in the paper. For the cat."

Merrill looked at her, his eyebrows going up slightly. "The cat? Are you sure it's still there? From what you said—"

"I'm not a hundred percent sure, no," she admitted, "but that doesn't make any difference. It's around the house somewhere—or it has been for two days—so there's no reason to think it will go away now. Maybe when we locate the owner, he can coax it out into the open."

Merrill was silent for a moment, his face expressionless behind the beard.

"All right," he said finally. "Tell Floyd what you want in the ad. I'll take care of it."

Again she started to protest, but thought better of it. Whatever Merrill's motives were, every little bit of money saved would be a help. And who was to say his motives weren't exactly what they seemed to be? Don't fight it *too* hard, she told herself, just be a little careful.

At lunch, at a small restaurant a few doors from the Journal, Merrill seemed preoccupied until, about halfway through the meal, Sorina decided that now was as good a time as any to bring up the problem of the missing papers. When she mentioned them, saying that she was running into a little difficulty, a frown creased his forehead, as if the mere thought of the papers was unpleasant.

"What sort of difficulty?"

She hesitated, slightly taken aback at the sudden

change in Merrill's mood. "I just have a couple of questions about the papers, that's all."

He nodded, but his eyes were averted, and he seemed to be concentrating on something beyond her field of vision.

"Go ahead," he said. "I don't guarantee any answers, though. As you may have gathered, I am not especially interested in this project my brother put up the money for."

"Yes, I had gathered that. But what I've never understood is why you're against it."

He was silent for several seconds before he replied, his eyes still not meeting hers.

"Any number of reasons," he said. "For one thing, it's too much like a vanity press to suit me. Paying to get your good deeds—if any—publicized."

"The Howalds did quite a bit, from what I've seen so far," Sorina said. "One congressman, an influential newspaper publisher, prominent businessman, and so on."

And why, she wondered even as she spoke, am I suddenly defending the Howalds against a member of their own family?

"In any event," she went on, "it's not a bad idea to get it down on the record, whether it's spectacular or not. That's what history is all about."

Again there was a long silence. "Yes," he said finally, a touch of resignation in his voice, "maybe you're right. Now, what was it you wanted to know?"

"The main question is, do you know if the papers out at West House are complete?"

"Complete?" He shrugged. "Those cabinets and boxes looked big enough to hold the papers for a half dozen families."

"I know they looked that way, but have you ever actually gone through them?"

"Hardly. As I said—"

"I know. You don't approve." And she wondered: Could that be where the missing papers had gone?

Could Merrill have gotten at them first? Could he have deliberately removed the bulk of them?

But she didn't ask him. Instead, she said, "Aside from two file cabinets full of your grandfather's papers from his time in Congress, there's very little in those cabinets and boxes except lots of neatly labeled folders. It looks as if the bulk of the papers, if they ever existed, are missing."

He shrugged. "According to the will, there was supposed to be a complete set of correspondence, personal and business, for every Howald who ever lived in Elston."

"That may very well be what the will says, but if the correspondence in those cabinets is complete, your family must have been even worse letter writers than I am."

"Perhaps you're right. I wouldn't know. As I have said so often—" He stopped, falling silent as a thin smile crossed his lips.

"I may have a solution to your little puzzle," he said, and Sorina could hear a humorless laugh in his voice. "The rest of the papers just haven't been sorted and filed yet."

Sorina frowned. "Then where are they?"

"I'm sure I don't know. I imagine Abel must have put them somewhere. He just hadn't gotten around to filing them yet—although your 'neatly labeled folders' makes it sound as if he had at least started organizing them. He probably knew what was supposed to go into each folder, but he just never got around to it. After all," he went on, bitterness edging its way into his voice, "he thought he had plenty of time left. Say another thirty or forty years. He wasn't in any great hurry."

Now it was Sorina's turn to be silent, and she wondered why she hadn't thought of something as obvious as that herself. When someone is in his thirties, he may make out his will just as a formality, but he doesn't really prepare for death. And in a case like this, where he would have had to sort through thousands of papers, not only of his own but of the past two generations . . .

"I'm sorry," she said finally, "I hadn't thought."

"It's all right," he said, and his bass voice was unexpectedly soft now, almost conciliatory. "I didn't think of it myself until right now."

She nodded. "I wonder where they are, though. Even if they weren't all sorted, they must be somewhere."

He shook his head. "I have no idea," he said, and a touch of sharpness—or was it nervousness?—had returned to his voice. "I haven't lived here for more than ten years. Why don't you talk to Ed Handley? He's the executor for the estate. He would have a better idea than I do, certainly."

The words signaled the end of the conversation, and she knew she would get no more from him, not right now at least.

The library was a square, brick building with a flat roof. Except for the numerous windows and the dozen steps leading up to the front door, it looked vaguely like a blockhouse. Inside, Merrill started for the desk, where a small, middle-aged woman was stamping a huge stack of books for a short, chubby girl with long, curly hair. As the woman stamped each one, the girl slid it into a shopping bag she carried with her.

Hollyhock, Sorina thought, if the cartoonist ever let her get old enough to enter junior high.

As Merrill went to the desk, Sorina looked around, located the card catalog, and motioned for him to follow. As it turned out, the only book that held any promise was a garish, purple thing, *The Gem Kingdom*, in the library's reference section. They settled themselves at the large, round table and began.

Their first guess at the stone, a garnet, was easily proved wrong. The photo of the garnet showed it to be far too red, with touches of yellow showing through some of the facets. On the same page as the garnet was another stone that looked closer, but not much—labradorite feldspar. Further on they found an orange opal, rather like a large blob of orange gelatin with sparkling green specks in it. A few dark spots in the opal looked to be about the shade she was looking for, but that was all.

Spinel was a deep, ruby red, much too dark and rich, and tourmaline, while it had a rusty tinge to it, was still wrong. For a moment, with the Spanish topaz, she thought she had found it, but, as with the opal, it was only a few facets that were the right shade. The rest of the gem was much too red, with very little brown.

Finally, in one corner of a set of paintings, she found it. A shade of reddish brown that could be described depending on your mood, as like that of a dark orange peel or dried blood. Light and dark specks were scattered like dust throughout the gem. Sorina scanned quickly through the legend at the bottom of the page.

"Carnelian," she said. "This is it, I'm sure. The shape is nothing like this, but everything else fits. It's carnelian."

"You're positive?"

"Yes—well, almost. If it's in this book at all, this is it." She stopped, frowning. "But what's carnelian? It's one I never heard of, any more than I heard of—what was that other one? Labradorite feldspar?"

"Something like that. But you're sure there's no mistake about this? Carnelian?"

"Reasonably sure, but I wouldn't bet my life on it. Why? Is it unusually valuable?"

He shook his head. "I don't think so. It's one of the alternate birthstones for August. It . . ."

She looked at him oddly as his voice trailed off, but said nothing. He seemed slightly ill at ease, and the beginnings of a frown creased his forehead. She wondered, did that kind of stone, a carnelian, have a special significance to him? A significance he wasn't willing to admit? Her mind went back to the first evening she had been in West House, and her first meeting with Merrill Howald. He had seemed suspicious of something then, too. He had, she remembered, asked the same question a number of times: Was she *sure* she didn't know Norris Amers?

And now the same not-quite-satisfied look was in his eyes, as if, for whatever reason, he didn't quite believe her, but was not doubtful enough to come right out and accuse her of something.

But what could there be about a carnelian—or an imitation carnelian, if there were such things—in a cat's collar that would concern anyone? Anyone except whoever had to pay for it, of course.

"What shape did you say the stone was?" Merrill asked after the silence between them had stretched on for at least a half minute.

"The main facet was a narrow oval," Sorina said. "I didn't see anything like it in this book, except . . ."

She flipped through several pages, coming to a stop at a large, pinkish-gray stone.

"Vaguely like this one, except the sides are curved instead of straight." She looked at the caption beneath the picture. "And this one, they say, is 'oddly cut.' I suppose that means the one in the collar is even more 'oddly cut.' "

Merrill looked down at the picture. "Yes, I suppose it does," he said softly, and Sorina could detect a slight hardening of his features. "I suppose it does."

After calling Ed Handley, the estate executor, and getting his promise to "look into" the supposedly missing papers, of which he disclaimed all knowledge, Sorina spent what little was left of the afternoon plowing through more of Leroy Howald's Congressional file. She had another dozen of her file cards done by the time the doorbell rang at about five o'clock. At least those four years in Washington would be well covered, she thought as she walked down the hall toward the door. It's just too bad the congressman never did anything that was particularly spectacular.

When she opened the door, Norris Amers was standing there, holding a copy of the *Elston Journal* in one hand.

"Just delivered," he said, handing it to her. "Thought I'd bring it up, since it's such a long walk to your mailbox."

She looked blank for a moment before she realized what he was talking about, and then she remembered the mailbox down by the road, near the end of the drive. For someone who had always lived in one city or another, where mailboxes were slots in doors or metal rectangles in apartment house hallways, having a mailbox on a metal post nearly a half block away was something new. Why, she wondered, hadn't the Howalds, with all their money, been able to get their mail delivered right to the door? But, then, that was probably what servants were for.

"Thanks," she said, glancing at the headlines. She looked back at Amers, who was standing quietly and watching her. "Would you care to come in for a minute?"

"I was hoping you'd ask," he said, moving aside quickly, as if to cross the threshold before Sorina could change her mind. "How are things going?"

She shrugged. "A little slow right now," she said noncommittally.

"I imagine it will be quite a job," he went on. "I saw all those boxes and filing cabinets when they moved them in. I suppose they're all crammed full."

"Some of them are," she said.

"Yes, well, it'd be too much for me, I'm afraid. But I suppose you're used to doing research like this. School and everything."

She nodded. "I've done my share."

"I can imagine. I only went to college for two years myself, but I got enough of it to last me a good, long time." He smiled. "I suppose most of these Howald things are business records and the like."

"Some," she said. "Right now I'm going through the ancient history. All the papers old Leroy Howald saved from his two terms in Congress."

The smile faded slightly. "Yes, I imagine he saved quite a lot, even though his record as a legislator wasn't overly distinguished, as I understand it."

She shrugged. "Possibly not. I haven't seen anything spectacular in the papers yet, at any rate."

"I doubt that you will," Amers said, and the smile returned, although it did not seem quite as boyish as it had before. "But, then, Representatives don't start making a splash until they've been around Washington for a dozen terms or so. And Leroy only managed two."

There seemed to be a touch of satisfaction in Amers' voice.

"Well, it's hard to get a picture of someone from correspondence like that," Sorina said, and then paused thoughtfully. "Mr. Amers, I—"

"Not 'Mr. Amers,' please. Just Norris."

"All right. Norris, then. Do you know any local people who might remember Leroy Howald? Some people who actually knew him?"

"I'm sure there are some. He's only been dead since when? Sometime in the 1920s, wasn't it?"

She nodded. "He died in 1925. But his terms in Congress were about twenty years earlier."

"Your best bet is the people you're working for, the Historical Society. If anyone knows, they should. Don't you think?"

"You're probably right. I'll ask them tomorrow." She shrugged. "Maybe they don't want me to do any interviewing yet, though. But it can't hurt to ask."

"If there's anything else I can do . . ." Amers let his voice trail away.

"I know," Sorina said, smiling, "just give you a call.

Incidentally, do you know of anyone in the neighborhood whose cat is missing?"

Amers blinked at the abrupt change of subject. "Cat? No, I haven't heard of any. Why do you ask?"

"There's one in this house. Or there was. It may have gotten out."

"Probably just a stray," Amers said, "or one that was dumped off. People are doing that all the time around here."

"Not this one. It has a collar, an expensive one with a gem in it. It's more like a necklace than a collar, actually."

Amers frowned thoughtfully. "I can't imagine whose it would be. What kind of cat is it?"

"Long hair, mostly white with some patches of orange and tan. No particular breed."

Amers shook his head. "I draw a complete blank. I don't own a cat, and the Hennings—they're the first house in the other direction—have a couple, but none of them look like that. And they certainly wouldn't spend the money for a fancy collar."

"Yes, it does seem a little strange. I had my hands on the animal for a while last night, trying to find some identification on the collar. But there wasn't any. And when I tried to take the collar off, it went wild and got away."

"Is it still in the house?"

"I don't know. I don't see how it could have gotten out, unless— Are there any special doors in the house for cats or dogs to use by themselves?"

"None that I know of, but I suppose it's possible. Clarice—Mrs. Howald—had some cats she was very attached to."

"Yes, that's what Merrill said this afternoon. He said that one of his sisters, who lives a couple of hundred miles from here, had taken the cats."

Amers nodded, and Sorina wondered if she could detect a certain stiffness in his motion or his words.

"Etta," he said, "or maybe Emma, her name is. I

don't remember her last name, but I could find out . . ."

"No reason to," Sorina said. "Unless this could be one of her cats that somehow managed to find its way back here. Stranger things have happened."

"It doesn't sound like it," Amers assured her. "None of her cats looked like the one you described."

"I didn't really think it was possible anyway," Sorina admitted. "But still, it has to have come from somewhere. Maybe we'll find out this evening. I put an ad in the *Journal* describing the cat and the collar."

"What kind of gem is in the collar? Or is it just plastic?"

"I'm pretty sure it's genuine, or else a very good imitation. I think it's a carnelian."

"Carnelian? I'm not familiar with that stone."

"I wasn't either, until we—Merrill and I—looked it up at the library. It's sort of rusty red, a mixture of red and brown. And this one—although they're not all that way, according to the book we found it in—had dozens of tiny spots, both light and dark, deep inside it. And the shape was unusual, too, almost as if it had been made for the cat—which I assume it was."

"Unusual? In what way?"

"It was an elongated oval, sort of like the pupil in a cat's eye."

"Yes, that does sound unusual," Amers said slowly, and for a moment he looked around the hallway, glancing toward the foot of the stairway, then toward the second floor.

"Very unusual," he went on after the long pause. "I don't suppose you noticed the collar itself?"

"As a matter of fact, I did. It was almost as unusual as the gem. I couldn't be sure, but it felt like velvet."

Amers' face remained expressionless. "Velvet, yes. Well, it does sound as if you have an unusual cat on your hands. If you *do* still have it on your hands."

"I know. I've been wondering the same thing myself. I haven't seen it since it disappeared last night, and it hasn't touched any of the food I left out for it."

"I see. Well . . ." He glanced at his watch. "I had better be moving on. I have to show someone a house in a half hour."

He turned toward the door, opened it, and paused with it still partially open. "It's been nice seeing you again, Miss Stark—Sorina. And if it's not too much trouble, let me know if the cat shows up again. Give me a call, in fact. I must admit that it has me intrigued, and I'd like to see it. If it's still here, of course."

"Of course," Sorina said. She could not help noticing that Amers had tensed up in the last few minutes, and she tried to remember just when it had happened. When she had mentioned the cat? The carnelian? The shape of the stone? She couldn't be sure, and as she tried to remember, Amers gave a peremptory wave and was gone.

After an early supper—one of the TV dinners she had gotten the day before—and a few words with Jenny Hanson on the phone, and while the sun was still a few degrees above the horizon, Sorina decided to take a look around the houses and grounds, thinking she might come across either the cat itself or some hole it could have escaped through.

But there was nothing, at least as far as feline escape routes went. All four doors leading out of West House—front and back in the central hall, the one from the kitchen to the passageway, and the one from the library to the garage—were all completely solid and, this time, firmly latched or locked.

As she stepped out the back door, she noticed that the brisk north wind that had been blowing most of the day had died down to a breeze and shifted to the west. The weather was still clear and crisp, but some of the chill seemed to have left.

The grounds in the back were at least three times the size of those in the front, stretching off to the north for the distance of a city block. Near the back were what had been a pair of large barns. The east one, according to Hunter, had been converted sometime in the thirties into a stable for raising horses, but the other had been unused for half a century and stood silent and neglected.

Directly behind West House, a hundred feet or so, was a gazebo, nestled in the middle of a near-maze of hedges, and off to the left Sorina could see what appeared to be a small tennis court. To the right, not far from the central house, were a few smaller buildings—toolshed, smokehouse, and the like—and between these buildings and the stable was an oval track, unfenced, presumably for use with the horses. A second, somewhat differently arranged mass of hedges with a central gazebo was behind East House, and behind that, taking up the northeast corner of the grounds, cut off from the rest by the same creek that meandered across the front lawn next to the road, was a large orchard. A single foot bridge crossed the stream into the orchard.

For a half hour Sorina wandered more or less aimlessly from one part of the grounds to another. The grass, though it hadn't been mowed in the last few weeks, was not so tall that it made walking difficult. Amers, she assumed, must have done whatever maintenance was necessary. If he was handling the land, trying to sell it, he would probably have to keep it at least presentable. Although who, she wondered, would buy a place like this? The two large houses, while oversize by most people's standards, were not totally out of the question for someone who had a fair amount of money and wanted a lot of leisurely country living. And the stable would be ideal for anyone who wanted to raise horses. But the third house, and the fact that all three were connected and shared common grounds would, she thought, make things more difficult. Unless, of course, Amers were to hold a one-cent sale, throwing in the second house (which, after all those years of disuse, could not be in all that great a shape) as a bonus. A few rooms could, she supposed, be fixed up as a guest house. Although with the number of guest rooms in West House, there was little reason to expect anyone would need a guest house. Still, why not? If you had the money to afford a place like this, you could also afford a lot of guests.

Oh, well, Sorina shrugged to herself. As far as she was concerned, the rich were a different breed entirely, and she would very likely never understand a single one of them.

Merrill Howald was certainly rich—or would be when the estate got settled, at least—and she certainly couldn't understand *him*. It bothered her the way his mood seemed to shift from minute to minute for no apparent reason. Was that the way rich people were? With money and security, they could afford the luxury of being erratic? Or could it be the effect of his brother's death? Had Merrill actually been closer to Abel than he had so far let on?

With the thought, her own mood shifted as rapidly as Merrill's ever had, and she wondered how she herself would feel if she were suddenly notified that her own brother, John, had died—or been murdered. These last few years they had been practically strangers, yet the sinking sensation that probed at her stomach told her that she could not take his death calmly, not calmly at all.

She shook her head sharply, forcing her thoughts toward other areas, back onto the history that she was supposed to be writing.

If she was going to do even a halfway decent job of it, she would have to gain some sort of understanding of the Howalds—who they were, why they did what they did, why they didn't do what they didn't do, etc. If the missing papers were found soon enough, they might give her a better picture. But if they weren't . . .

What she really needed was to talk to the people who had known the Howalds, who remembered what they and the country had been like sixty and seventy years ago. There must, she thought, be a few such people still living in the area. Tomorrow she would get their names from someone at the Society, and try to talk to a few of them. It would undoubtedly be more useful—and more interesting—than continuing to plod through the mass of Leroy Howald's Congressional papers.

She was not far from the stables, about to start back toward the houses before the last traces of twilight disappeared, when a movement caught her eye. She looked toward the creek that wandered back onto the grounds and formed the nearly rectangular boundary between the orchard and the rest of the land. It was there, not far from the narrow bridge, that she had spotted the movement. Something small and quick, like—

A cat?

Sorina frowned and started walking toward the bridge. The sun was dropping below the horizon to the west, and the light was fading rapidly, particularly here, where a half dozen oak and willow trees blocked the reddish glow that still covered the western rim of the sky.

Then she saw it. It *was* the cat! It sat in the taller grass along the creek bank, just to one side of the bridge, a spot of white in the deepening shadows.

Sorina moved toward it slowly, trying not to look threatening, and wondering if talking to it would do any good. When she was within a half dozen yards, it got up quickly, its eyes never leaving Sorina, and trotted across the bridge to the orchard. On the far side it stood waiting, eying Sorina expectantly.

As Sorina stepped onto the bridge, the animal turned again and started back into the orchard, moving easily through the grass that was inches taller than itself.

Sorina stopped, glanced again toward the fading glow in the west.

"Not today, cat," she said finally as she turned on the bridge and started back toward the houses, "not without my trusty flashlight."

She glanced back once, and the only evidence of the

cat was the movement of some grass a dozen yards from the bridge.

Well, Sorina thought as she moved back toward the houses, so much for the captive cat. Obviously it had its own way in and out of the house. But where? None of the doors had any openings for it. And certainly the windows couldn't have been made so that a cat could open and close them.

Could there be an open window somewhere? Maybe just a couple of inches, that was all it would take. A cat could squirm through an opening that, just looking at it, you wouldn't think possible. And the weather hadn't been cold enough yet for the draft from a single open window to be noticed.

Yes, that must be it, a window, and Sorina couldn't imagine why she hadn't thought of such an obvious solution before.

As she approached the backs of the houses, she saw that she was much closer to East House than to West House. On an impulse, she turned toward the east, cutting between East House and the hedges that surrounded the second gazebo. There was still enough light to see where she was going, so there was no reason she shouldn't go around this way and walk back along the front of the complex of houses to reach the front door of West House. She hadn't really gotten a good look at East House yet, and she wondered if it looked as much like West House up close as it did at a distance.

As far as she could tell, it did. It appeared to have the same number of windows in the same patterns, as well as the same flat roof and the same lines of gray, gloomy stone. The only difference seemed to be that East House was a mirror image of West House. The kitchen, connecting to the passageway, was presumably on the west end of the house, not the east. And the library . . .

As she passed the steps leading to the front door, she looked up at what she assumed was the library window. Wondering if her guess was right, she moved off the gravel drive onto the grass that separated it from the house.

As she approached, she saw there was another difference. The windows in this house were dirty, as if they hadn't been washed in years, and the paint on the windowsills and the door was cracked and peeling.

Not surprising, she thought, if it hadn't been occupied since Aaron Howald, Jr., sold out his interest in the estate and left, sometime in the 1920s. Actually, considering the house hadn't been lived in for nearly fifty years, it seemed to be in remarkably good shape.

She stepped over what had been flower beds many years before and stood on tiptoes to look in the window.

She gasped!

It *was* the library—and there was someone in it!

5

In an instant the figure was gone, and she wondered if she had really seen it.

It had been a dark figure, little more than a deeper shadow among a host of shadows, nearly all the way across the library, near the door to what she assumed was the dining room. And in the instant it had taken her to blink, it had disappeared.

Still on tiptoes, she pressed her face against the window, trying to keep the faint light from outside from preventing her from seeing into the deeply shadowed interior.

But there was nothing, no one. Whoever or whatever it had been—her own imagination? a reflection in the glass?—was gone.

She backed away from the window, glancing once more to the west, where the red had faded from a sky that was rapidly turning black. A half dozen stars were already winking into life.

No, she thought, it had been too dark for her to really see anything inside the house. It had just been her imagination, or . . . She glanced around as she returned to the gravel drive and walked toward West House, looking for a tree or bush whose reflection she might have seen in the glass in the window. There were a number of them, of course, but none were very close, and . . .

She shook her head. There was no point in speculating anymore; obviously it was an illusion of some sort, a reflection.

Unless . . .

Her mind went back to her first night at the house and her unexpected encounter with Merrill. Could *he* be wandering around the old house in the dark? But why?

With an irritated shake of her head—as much at her own fantasies as anything else—she continued determinedly along the drive to West House.

Back in the house, she called the Fairview and asked for Merrill's room. When there was no answer, she left a message for him to call her as soon as he came in. She wasn't sure precisely what good it would do, but it seemed like a good idea. Despite his shifting moods, there was something solid about him.

Next she dialed Norris Amers' number. It, too, rang unanswered.

So much for local assistance, she thought as she hung up. But, then, Norris had told her he was going to be showing a house to someone this evening. But that had been—she glanced at her watch—nearly three hours ago. It certainly shouldn't take that long.

On the other hand, she couldn't expect either of them to just sit around waiting for her to call.

She glanced around the office at the filing cabinets and boxes. How much material, beyond the Congressional papers, did they actually contain? She should, she supposed, get a more specific idea of what was actually here—as well as what was missing—before she began pushing Handley any harder to locate the missing papers.

Abel Howald's box was on top, she noticed. It was as good a place to start as any. She opened the flaps and flipped through the folders. What few letters there were—and there seemed to be more in this box than she remembered seeing in most of the others—were arranged in roughly chronological order within each folder. As she was going through a seemingly miscellaneous folder, she came across a letter from Merrill. It was about two years old and had been written primarily to tell Abel that he wasn't interested in coming back to Elston to occupy East House and help with the family business. For one thing, the house had been vacant for fifty years, and Merrill didn't feel like going to the trouble of getting all the work done that would be necessary before it could be lived in again. For another, he just wasn't interested in returning to Elston, period, businesses or no businesses. He also mentioned that he was doing quite all right where he was, and he saw no reason to make a change.

As Sorina replaced the letter, she wondered: Would Merrill stay in Elston now? If he did, after all, inherit the majority of the estate, he would just about have to stay. Although he could, she supposed, sell it. Or leave its management to someone else.

But Merrill Howald's plans weren't any of her business, she told herself, except insofar as they affected the work she was doing for the Historical Society. She had no personal interest, certainly.

Did she?

She shook her head. No, her job was strictly with the dead Howalds, not the live ones.

The dead Howalds . . .

With the thought, a touch of morbid curiosity arose within her, and she wondered what their last moments had been like. Had they known what was happening?

With a shudder, she replaced the folder in the box. Then, as she was debating whether to continue through other boxes or to just relax with one of the books she had brought with her, the doorbell sounded.

It was Merrill. He had gotten her message and decided to drive out to see her rather than just calling. He seemed to be, she was glad to note, in one of his pleasanter phases. He glanced around at the furniture, all still hidden beneath dust covers, and walked to the stairs.

He sat down on one of the broad steps, his long legs jackknifing so that his knees were almost on a level with his chin. He leaned back, propping his elbows on one of the higher steps.

Her eyes went involuntarily toward the spot next to the stairs, and the images of Abel and the others darted through her mind. But she forced them out and walked to the stairs to join Merrill. She leaned against the ornate railing on the opposite side.

"Now, what was it you called about?" he asked. "Not the papers again, I hope." He smiled to indicate, perhaps, that he was joking.

"No, not the papers. There was—" She stopped, began again. "Were you out here this evening? About an hour ago, say?"

He frowned in mock seriousness, or so it seemed. "No, why?"

"Nothing important, probably," she said. "I thought I saw someone in East House."

"Oh? And who might that have been?" Was it her imagination, or had a note of tension entered his voice?

"Probably no one. I was looking through one of the windows, and it was almost dark, so . . ." Her voice trailed off as she thought back to the brief glimpse she had gotten.

"Yes?" Merrill prompted.

"It was just a shape, a shadow, that's all. In the library of East House. But it was gone in a second. It was probably just my imagination."

"Did you go inside to look for it?"

"How? I don't have a key."

He shrugged. "Probably just as well. It must have been one of the ghosts."

In spite of herself, a shiver ran down her back. She had never believed in ghosts, not even as a child, not intellectually, yet the mention of them had always affected her that way.

"What ghosts?" she asked.

"Take your pick. My brother and his family would certainly have legitimate reasons to haunt the place, wouldn't you say? And Aaron and Leroy both died there back in the twenties, though their deaths were natural, not violent."

She searched his face, looking for an indication. "You're not serious, are you? About ghosts?"

"Why not?" He shrugged again, but his eyes were averted, looking first at the front door, then toward the darkened living room with its shrouded furniture. "Stranger things have happened, so they tell me."

"Possible," she said, "but I'm afraid I don't believe in ghosts." Her voice, she realized, displayed more confidence than she felt within herself.

"That's too bad. You're probably missing half the fun of living out here," he said, and she thought that she could detect a note of bitterness behind the light words and bland expression.

"But," he went on, "if you want something more solid than a spirit, have you thought about Norris Amers?"

"Amers? Why would he be skulking about?"

"I'm sure I don't know. But he does have the keys to the place—unless he gave them all to you."

"No, I have only those to West House. But what would he be doing out here—in the dark, no less?"

"Who knows? I certainly don't pretend to understand the workings of his mind. For that matter, what did you think *I* would be doing there?" He looked up at her, a faint smile appearing on his bearded face.

"No idea. I just remembered your sudden appearance the first night I was here."

"Yes," he said, the smile broadening, "I imagine that was a little startling. But no more startling to you than to me, I assure you. Incidentally, did you ever get in touch with Handley? About the missing papers?"

"Yes, for all the good it did."

"He couldn't help you?"

"He said he'd look into it, but he had no idea where any such papers might be—if they existed at all. He gave me the distinct impression that he thought their existence was extremely unlikely."

"He could be right, you know."

"But the will—"

"He could still be right. Maybe, after getting the material organized, Abel decided to drop the whole thing.

Maybe he threw out most of the material, and just never got around to changing the will. Don't forget, he thought he had plenty of time."

By now his smile had faded. A trace of bitterness came into his tone, as it had before when he had spoken of his brother's death, and his face grew somber.

A new thought entered Sorina's mind. Could Merrill be protecting Abel's memory? Could that be why he was against the history?

Merrill recovered quickly, however, and when he spoke again his voice was light. "In case the papers don't exist, and you find yourself with nothing to do for the next few weeks, don't forget those other job offers. They're still good."

"Thanks, I'll keep them in mind, but I think I'll hang around here a while longer." She stopped, looking at him thoughtfully. "What I don't understand is, why are you offering me these jobs? Is it worth that much to you to keep the history from being written?"

He blinked once, as if taken aback by her blunt question. Finally, he shrugged. "Possibly," he said, "but did it ever occur to you that I might have other motives?"

"Such as?"

"Such as, I might just like you, and think that you would do a good job, no matter what type of work you got into."

"I must admit the thought hadn't occurred to me."

"Well, you might start considering such possibilities. They're not totally out of the question, are they?"

"I suppose not. But you're not going to tell me that you wouldn't, just a little, like to get the history killed, are you?"

He smiled reluctantly. "No, I'm not. After all, I've told you a number of times how I felt about it, so . . ."

He stood up, uncoiling until he loomed over her. His hand brushed against her arm, and he looked down at her. "But I *do* like you, whether you believe me or not."

Their eyes met, and Sorina tried to see behind the mask, to see what his thoughts really were.

After a moment he started to lean down, then hesitated, a smile breaking across his face. He reached down, put his hands on her waist, and, with no apparent effort, lifted her and set her on the first step of the stairs.

Sorina was startled, but she did not draw back when he leaned forward and kissed her. And as he did, as she felt his lips moving lightly on hers, it came to her that this was her first kiss in more time than she liked to remember.

And she enjoyed it, and responded, pressing against him.

Even so, she couldn't keep the thought from her mind: Don't rush. That's what got you into trouble the first time. No contracts, not yet.

After a few seconds she drew back, and she wondered if her reservations showed in her face. Apparently they did. Merrill looked down at her silently and then, with a half smile, half shrug, put his hands around her waist again and effortlessly picked her off the step and set her back onto the hall floor.

"Being tall does have its disadvantages sometimes," he said, still smiling. "And now I suspect I had best be going."

He looked down at her, then turned toward the door. "Don't forget," he said, as the door swung open under his hand, "whatever my motives, the offer of a job still holds."

She stood silently as she heard his steps across the porch, then the sound of his car door closing and the engine starting.

All right, she said to herself, things could be looking up. At the very least, you're assured of a job, even if this one does fall through for lack of research material. At the very least, a job . . .

Right now, though, it might be a good idea to get busy. Call someone at the Historical Society, for instance, to see what they thought of her idea of talking to oldsters in the community, of collecting oral history.

A call to Jenny got her Mrs. Strickland's home number, and the opinion that, really, it was Barbara Strickland who ran the Society, not Hunter, despite the fact that he was its president. A figurehead, Jenny said, good for getting contributions.

Barbara Strickland was not only amenable to the idea of oral history, she was downright enthusiastic.

"Come on over," she said, "and I'll have a half dozen names for you to start with. And you can pick up my cassette, too, and a couple of tapes. All I ask is that you don't try too hard to limit these people to talking about the Howalds. Let them have their heads, so to speak."

Sorina agreed, and later in the evening drove to the Strickland house.

"We'll get something for this money yet," the older woman said as she handed the cassette and blank tapes to Sorina. "We've been doing this sort of thing for a couple of years now. Just having people who have lived here all their lives talk for as long as they want about how things used to be. One of the high-school history classes started it. It was a class project, and they got nearly a hundred hours of tape for us. Now if we can just get the five hundred or a thousand hours it will take to transcribe all those tapes . . ."

She looked questioningly at Sorina. "I don't suppose you'd care to volunteer a little time?"

Sorina shook her head. "Not for that. I type, but I don't take shorthand, which means I'll have more than enough trouble transcribing my own stuff."

"I see what you mean. Well, it can't hurt to ask, I always say. Incidentally, I saw your ad for the cat this evening. Any responses yet?"

"None, and I'm a little surprised. I still can't imagine a cat with a collar like that not being missed by someone. Although . . ." Sorina paused thoughtfully. "Maybe it's not missing at all."

"How do you mean? I thought you said it had been at the house ever since you arrived."

"It has been, but only now and then. It apparently has some way of getting in and out of the house by itself—though I'm damned if I can find out how it's doing it. It was inside last night, but it was outside today, and I swear I didn't leave any doors open. In fact, unless it lives on what it catches, it *must* be going home, at least to be fed. I've left cat food and milk out for it a couple of times, but it hasn't touched them."

"Why don't you check with your neighbors? There aren't all that many, and— Come to think of it, one of them is on your list. Bessie Platte. She lives just a half mile or so behind the Howald place, on the next road over."

Mrs. Strickland paused, thinking. "Amers, of course, you already know, just to the east of you. On the other side are the Hennings. And there's a Rogers—Tola, I think the name is—somewhere in the same area. There are a couple of others, but . . . Look, when you finish your interviews tomorrow, give me a call. Or better yet, stop by. You can tell me how they went, and I can give you the names of any other neighbors I can think of. And maybe the names of a few more people for you to interview . . ."

Sorina laughed as Mrs. Strickland's voice trailed off suggestively. "Why not? If Handley doesn't come up with the rest of the papers, I'm not going to have a great deal to do out at the Howald place after a few more days."

"Oh? What papers?"

"I'm sorry, I should have told you. Or asked you, rather. It's beginning to look as if that collection of Howald papers is pretty skimpy. The only thing that's fully documented is Leroy Howald's time in Congress."

Mrs. Strickland looked puzzled. "But all those file cabinets . . . And the boxes!"

"That's what I thought at first, too, but did you ever look inside the cabinets and boxes? Closely?"

The older woman shook her head. "As a matter of fact, no. Handley just pointed them out to me. 'These are the papers,' he said, that sort of thing. You mean there wasn't anything in them?"

"Not a lot. A great many neatly labeled folders, but very little in the folders."

Sorina frowned as she remembered the suspicion that had crossed her mind earlier.

"Is it possible," she asked, "that Merrill Howald took some of the papers?"

"Merrill? I don't understand."

"I don't either, but it's occurred to me that since Merrill is so set against this family history project, he might have taken the papers, just to insure that it never gets off the ground."

"Merrill *against* the project? Now I *really* don't understand! The only time I talked to him, the day Handley told us about the will, he seemed quite enthusiastic."

"Oh? Are you sure we're talking about the same person? Merrill Howald? About six-three, slender, with a reddish beard?"

"That's him, but . . ." Mrs. Strickland shook her head. "I just don't see what's going on. I don't remember his exact words, but he was definitely in favor of the project."

"Maybe it's just me," Sorina said. "I mean, if he was all in favor of the history the day before you hired me, and now he's turning thumbs down on it . . ."

Her mind went back to Merrill's final words earlier that evening: "Whatever my motives, the offer of a job still holds."

Whatever his motives . . .

"I wouldn't worry about it," Mrs. Strickland's voice broke into Sorina's brief reverie. "According to the will, Merrill doesn't have anything to say about it. It's all spelled out in the will."

She stopped for a moment, and a grin spread across

her face. "And if he just plain refuses to cooperate, or if he really is hiding some of the papers—well, we've got the money, and there's nothing he can do about *that*. And as I keep saying, there are a dozen other things you can be doing the next three months. Dozens . . ."

The cat made another appearance that night. As before, it awakened her by jumping onto the foot of the bed sometime after midnight. At least she assumed that was what had awakened her. She felt the pressure on her feet as she awoke, and then, after a moment of disorientation, saw the faintly glowing spots that were its eyes—and the carnelian.

She blinked a couple of times, and then, squinting her eyes protectively, switched on the bedside lamp. The cat, as if it had been waiting for its cue, leaped from the bed and darted for the door to the hall. When Sorina made no motion to follow, it sat just outside the door and stared back into the room.

Its mouth moved slightly, and a faint, almost inaudible mewing reached Sorina's ears.

"Not tonight, cat," Sorina said, wondering what it was about cats that made otherwise sane people want to talk to them, knowing full well that they couldn't understand a word, usually not even their names. "You just go slip back through whatever crack you've found and go home. I'm not going to follow you around tonight."

The cat mewed again, a little louder, and it made a motion to come back through the door.

"If you're going to be that way, you can just stay out." Sorina threw back the covers and climbed out of bed.

Instantly the cat was on its feet. moving away down the hall. Sorina, not bothering with her slippers, went to the door and started to push it shut.

"Let's see you get through this," she said to the spot of white that was the cat disappearing down the hall.

Then, as the door was almost closed, there was another sound. Not the mewing of the cat, not the sound of its nails on the hardwood floor as it ran, but something else.

Something else . . .

For a moment she stood silently, listening, the beginnings of a chill spreading over her as her mind involuntarily called up the image of the shadowy figure she had seen in East House.

But no, that was nonsense.

The door? Was the noise just the squeaking of her door as she swung it shut?

Experimentally, she swung the door open again, pushed it shut. At one point in the motion there was a faint grating sound, and at another the hinges squeaked a tiny bit.

But there was nothing like the sound she had just—heard?

It came again, louder this time—or was it just that she was now listening for it and it sounded louder in her ears?

And again. A moan?

Nonsense! her mind told her again, firmly, and yet the chill that had begun moments before became icy and dug at the middle of her back.

Leaving the door to the hall open, she went quickly back to the bed, pushed her feet into her slippers, and shrugged into the terrycloth robe. Its protective warmth took some of the chill away, but the spot in the middle of her back remained, a pulsing spot of tingling cold.

The sound came again as she moved toward the door, and this time she was sure it was a moan. Distant and sad, and yet . . .

Before stepping all the way into the hall, she reached around the door frame, ran her fingers along the wall until she found the light switch, and flipped it on. A spot of white disappearing over the top steps at the end of the hall was the only evidence of the cat.

Standing outside the door, she listened, and the sound came yet again.

A moan, long and drawn out . . .

Or was it the wind? The wind, moaning through some unseen crevice in the house—perhaps through the same crevice, she thought suddenly, that the cat had found. She didn't really believe it, but she could think of nothing else.

She glanced around the room once, and her eyes fell on the flashlight, lying on the bureau. She walked back and picked it up, tested the switch, and dropped it into the pocket of her robe. Somehow it gave her a feeling of security as she moved back into the hall. It was something solid, something she could hold in her own hands and control.

At first she moved slowly, pausing to listen every few steps, but then, as she approached the top of the stairs, she threw back her shoulders and pushed ahead at a normal pace. At the head of the stairs, she snapped on the downstairs lights.

Despite her determination, her steps faltered briefly as she descended the stairs, her hand on the railing. The sounds—the moans—seemed to be coming from directly below her, and they were clearer, more distinct than ever.

Impossible! It couldn't be happening, she told herself, and yet it was. And as she moved down the stairs, images swam through her mind, images of blood and death that she could not force away.

As she reached the bottom, she moved slowly around one side of the staircase and faced the rear of the house, not looking down, keeping her eyes up, away from the carpet.

And the moans continued. Finally, she looked down.

She sucked in her breath sharply, automatically telling herself that the faint spots on the carpet by the side of the stairs were simply in her mind. The light was poor here, and there were shadows, that was all.

She shivered, but she continued moving. There was, of course, a rational explanation for all of this. A rational, sane explanation, if only she could find it.

She stopped a few feet from the nearest spot—shadow—on the carpet. She pulled the flashlight from the pocket of her robe and flipped it on. The spot in the carpet seemed to fade, and yet . . .

As she looked, she realized that the moans had stopped. In the silence there was only the sound of her own breathing, and the pounding of her heart.

The cat, she wondered suddenly, where had the cat disappeared to this time? She swung the flashlight around, past the staircase toward the unlighted rooms beyond, then down the shadowy hallway that led to the back door.

But it was nowhere. It had vanished, along with the moans.

Then there was another sound. sharper, a sudden snap or click, from somewhere directly ahead of her. She jerked the flashlight upward, pointing it down the hall toward the sound.

For an instant she saw it, just an instant—a face, outlined in the glass in the back door, half hidden by the reflected glare of the flashlight itself.

And in that instant the figure she thought she had seen—*had* seen—in East House earlier in the evening took on a frightening reality.

6

Then, as abruptly as it had appeared, it was gone. Just as the figure in East House had vanished, the face disappeared, leaving only a faint afterimage in her eyes.

Suddenly the paralysis that had gripped her was also gone, and she darted forward, down the short hallway to the door, keeping the flashlight trained on the window all the way. As she reached the door, she snapped on the outside light, and the shrubs and trees within fifty feet of the door became visible. She grasped the knob and turned it.

But nothing happened.

The locks! Those damned double locks! And her keys were upstairs, on the bureau!

She pressed her face tightly against the glass, but could see nothing. There was no motion, no light other than the one she had just turned on.

Except . . .

Sorina burst out laughing, but the laugh was not wholly one of amusement or even of relief, and it was with difficulty that she controlled herself. Standing near the corner of the house, in what would have been a regal pose except that it kept looking over its shoulder toward the door, was the cat. Slowly, as Sorina's nervous laughter subsided, it moved off into the darkness.

There were no more sounds, no more feline appearances that night, and the cat was nowhere in evidence when Sorina awakened in the morning. Similarly, the spots she thought she had seen on the rug around the staircase were gone.

The memory of the sounds—and the face in the window—remained, however, and no morning rationalizations could remove them. Nor could she suppress a slight shudder whenever she thought of her dashing to the door and trying to throw it open to whoever—or whatever—had been there only moments before. She had been lucky, perhaps, that the locked door had prevented her from actually doing it. Still, she thought, she would probably do it again, although she hoped she would not be given the opportunity a second time. When she was confronted with something unusual or frightening, she tended to face up to it rather than turn and run. It would have been far easier, four years ago, to give in to Vern's demands, or at least to appear to give in to them for the time being. Later she could have continued to reason with him, tried to get him to see things her way.

But she had not. When it had finally become clear in her mind that he was not going to live up to his part of the bargain willingly, she had taken most of the few hundred dollars that had been in their joint savings account—since she had earned most of it while Vern had been going to school, she felt she was entitled to at least that much—and left.

She had often wondered if this tendency to charge ahead almost regardless of consequences was wise, but she had never consciously tried to curb it. She had decided that whatever problems it caused her were probably smaller than the problems that would have been caused by hesitancy or indecision. Whatever the problems turned out to be, she would find them out immediately. Deferring them to a later date by rationalizing or procrastinating only made them worse, no matter what they were. For the last four years this tendency was all that had kept her going through many a long winter night when she had spent eight hours waiting tables only to come back to her room at three in the morning to put in four more hours of studying before catching a couple of hours sleep before her first class. If she had ever hesitated, put something off and simply said, "I'll do it tomorrow," she would never have made it.

And the way she had taken this job was another example. Interviewed, accepted, and started, all in one day. There were, she knew, times when she would have been better off to take her time and think things over, but she doubted that she would ever make a policy of it. Although, she had to admit, she was being relatively cautious regarding Merrill Howald. But, then, after the disaster she had gotten into with Vern Malloy, perhaps men were one category in which she *had* developed a cautious outlook.

The first half hour of the morning she spent checking the ground around the back of the entire house, looking for she knew not what and finding nothing, and then making a quick tour of the entire house on the inside, checking all the windows on both floors and in the basement. There were none that were open even a crack, let alone the two or three inches necessary for the cat to get through.

After that she spent a little time with the Congressional papers, then she made another call to Ed Handley. He was no more help this time than he had been the evening before. His only new suggestions was that, since Abel had maintained files in the offices of each of the dozen businesses he had owned, it was possible, though unlikely, that the missing papers were in one of those offices. He would, he assured her, check into it at the first opportunity.

Sorina spent most of the rest of the day talking to some of the people on the list Mrs. Strickland had given her. By late afternoon she had more than three hours of tape, but very little of it had any value for the Howald family history. Most of it, however, seemed to be just the sort of thing that Mrs. Strickland was after, and a lot of it was, whether it was useful or not, rather interesting.

The only person who had much to say about the Howalds was Bessie Platte, who had been an elementary-school teacher from about 1900 until she had retired sometime in the 1950s. She hadn't known either Leroy or Aaron, Sr., very well, but she had taught both Martin and Aaron, Jr., from the first to the fourth grade.

"We were one of the few two-room schools in the state, so far as I know," Miss Platte said, once she had gotten used to Sorina's pointing the microphone at her each time she started to say something. "Aaron was two years ahead of Martin. They were nice enough children, considering who they were. I was surprised they went to public school, myself. With the kind of money their fathers had—well, there were a lot of parents who had less money who still sent their children away to private schools."

She smiled in recollection, a tiny gnome of a woman, hair pulled back in a tight bun. "They were probably—what is the term they use nowadays? Building their image? It was about then that Leroy went to Congress and Aaron started sounding political in his editorials. And it wouldn't have looked good for them to send their children to private schools. Not democratic."

And, a little later in the interview: "They got along with most of the other children. I imagine they were under strict orders from their parents on that subject. 'Don't pick fights with the children of potential voters.' Or perhaps I've become too cynical these last few years. Lord knows I didn't think that at the time. Or perhaps I'm just a little jealous. My father was one of the candidates Leroy Howald defeated for that second term in Congress."

The old woman smiled reminiscently. "But they weren't *always* on their best behavior. I remember there was one boy—no, two boys, two brothers, it was. Their name was Amers. Jack and Harold, I think. They were always fighting with the two Howald boys."

"Amers? Were they related to Norris Amers?" Sorina asked.

"Little Norris? Yes, I had him in school, too. That

must have been just after the war. The second one, I mean. I had only the first and second grades then."

"Is he related to Jack and Harold?"

"He's Harold's son. I think. It's hard to keep a half century of faces straight in my mind sometimes. Especially the more recent ones. The first ones, when I was just starting, just out of school myself, are easy."

For a moment her eyes were back there with her "first ones," in Portman County's only two-room schoolhouse. By the time she was finished she had filled nearly a full ninety-minute tape, but there was little more that related to either the Howalds or the Amers.

And she had no idea who the cat might belong to.

Later in the afternoon, as Sorina was leaving eighty-five-year-old Art Weaver with another half-hour tape of turn-of-the-century reminiscences that had little to do with the Howalds, she realized she was only a half mile from the Portman County State Prison Farm. She thought for a moment of calling on another of the oldsters on Mrs. Strickland's list, but a glance at her watch dissuaded her. It was late afternoon, probably suppertime for most of them, so they could wait for another day. In the meantime it seemed a shame to waste the opportunity to get a closer look at the prison farm. For one thing, though she had known of its existence most of her life, she had never been close to it and had little idea of how it worked or what it looked like. And if, as had been hinted, she was going to include a fairly large section on the deaths themselves in the history, she should at least take the time to become familiar with the place from which the murderer had escaped. In any event, she realized as she drove toward the small gray building that, according to the sign, was prison farm headquarters, she was interested in it herself.

John Ormand, the warden, turned out to be more than willing to talk about the incident and to defend the prison-farm system at great length.

"For one thing, it's almost self-supporting. We grow a fair amount of our own food, and we sell a great deal of it, just as they do on any farm. For another, it's a hell of a lot more healthy than most prisons. Here the prisoners work outdoors almost every day. We don't just walk them out into some 'exercise yard' a couple times a day and let them shuffle around in a circle a few times."

When she asked Ormand about the ease with which the prisoners could escape, he was equally ready to defend the farm's minimum security setup.

"You've got to realize," he said, "that the prisoners we have here are virtually all what would be called trustees anywhere else. They aren't sent here if anyone thinks they'll try to escape."

"But they do escape sometimes."

Omand shrugged. "Sometimes, but not often. And often as not, they come back voluntarily. We rarely lose one permanently."

"But you do once in a while."

"Not as often as regular prisons, by quite a bit. And if you're talking about Barlow again, that was a freak case. Really a freak case."

"In what way?"

"In all kinds of ways. Just what do you already know about it?"

"Just what I read in the paper. I understand he was to be released in a few months."

"That's right, he was. Six, as a matter of fact. So he didn't have any reason to try to escape." Ormand shook his head. "There had to be something more to it than there appeared to be."

"For instance?"

Ormand hesitated. "For instance—do you know *how* he escaped?"

"Not precisely. From what I've heard, it's not too hard."

"No, it's not. It was especially easy for Barlow. He was a trustee, which means that even among the prisoners we have here, he was considered exceptionally trustworthy. We—Bob Crozier was warden then—would even send Barlow in to Elston on errands."

"Without a guard?"

"What's the point in sending a prisoner if you have to send a guard with him? We could send the guard by himself. But yes, without a guard. There are a half dozen or so we trust that much around here."

"What happened? Did he just drive away?"

"No. That's one of the things that's wrong about it. The prison car was parked in Elston. We found it that evening. The keys were missing. We never did find them."

"So? Someone must have—" She stopped, puzzled.

"Someone must have met him? Is that what you were going to say, Miss Stark?"

She nodded. "It was. But . . . If someone met him, what was he doing at the Howald's house? When was that, by the way?"

"They *say* he showed up at the Howald place the same evening."

"You don't think he did?"

"Frankly, no."

"What, then?"

"I don't think he *went* anywhere." From the tone of Ormand's voice, it was obvious that this was one of his favorite topics.

"What's that supposed to mean?" she asked.

"I don't think he had anything to do with the Howalds. I think he was kidnaped, and probably killed."

Sorina blinked, puzzled. "By whom? Why?"

"Maybe by one or more of the brothers of the man he had killed. They were a mean bunch, and they were the only ones at Barlow's trial that thought he should have gotten a stronger sentence. Everyone else thought he should have gotten a medal."

"But what about the Howalds? Didn't they find Barlow's prison clothes in the house?"

Ormand shrugged. "Not exactly."

"But I was told—"

"To be exact, they were found on the Henning place, a quarter of a mile to the west, out in a woods. Their little girl, Joetta, found them a week later. She came dragging them home one day."

"But if Barlow didn't kill the Howalds, how did his clothes get there?"

"The brothers again, maybe. Maybe they wanted it to look like Barlow killed them."

Sorina shook her head. "It doesn't sound very likely."

Ormand shrugged. "Maybe not. But it sounds as likely as Barlow taking a prison car into Elston, leaving it there, where it's sure to be found, finding a gun somewhere, walking nearly five miles to the Howald place, and killing them all for no reason other than to get a few dollars and a change of clothes. Hell, if he wanted clothes, he must've passed a dozen clotheslines between Elston and the Howald place."

Sorina frowned. "But if what you say is true, then who killed the Howalds?"

"It's possible the brothers did, but . . . I don't know. If Abel's brother hadn't been in California at the time, I'd have figured he was a good bet. But as it is, I just don't have any good ideas. All I know is, it doesn't make sense for Barlow to have done it. And where did he get to after he killed them? He just vanished without a trace. None of his relatives have ever heard from him, not a single word. And no one ever saw him, either. And believe me, we had enough posters of him circulated." He shrugged. "They're still up, for that matter, all over the state. Including here, just so we'll recognize him if he ever comes back."

Ormand nodded toward a large bulletin board on one wall of his office. A dozen pictures were tacked to it, and Sorina turned to study them. After a moment she found the one labeled "William Barlow." A square face, deepset eyes, high cheekbones, straight dark hair cut very short.

Sorina frowned. And she thought: I've seen that face.

I've seen that face, but where? And when?

7

Back at West House, while she was waiting for another TV dinner to heat up, Sorina called Mrs. Strickland, who was, if not overjoyed, at least greatly pleased with what Sorina said was on the tapes.

"I'm sorry you didn't get more information on the Howalds, though," the older woman said.

"That's all right, I got a little. And I think Miss Platte will probably remember more if I give her a chance. She might even have a few letters of her father's, from the time he ran against Leroy Howald for Congress."

"Oh, yes, I'd forgotten about that. But it wasn't much of a contest. It wasn't that Leroy was a great congressman or even a great speaker, from what I've heard. Orin Platte just wasn't cut out for public service."

"One interesting thing she mentioned, though," Sorina said, "was about Norris Amers' father and uncle. She said they and the two Howald boys were always fighting, almost like a family feud. Do you know anything about that?"

There was a brief silence, and when Mrs. Strickland spoke again, her voice was hesitant.

"Not between them, specifically," she said finally.

Sorina frowned. "Between some other members of the family? Is that what you mean? Like Norris Amers and Abel Howald?"

"No, not that. It was— Well, I wasn't going to tell you. I didn't want to give you any preconceived ideas. After all, that's why we were required to hire someone from outside the county in the first place."

"Tell me what?" Sorina prodded when Mrs. Strickland fell silent.

"That there was a feud of sorts between the Howalds and the Amers, but it started between Leroy and Aaron and Norris's grandfather, Simon Amers. I don't know any of the details, of course, just that they had a falling out. Simon was a partner with them, but they broke the partnership sometime in the 1890s."

"Do you know why?"

"Nobody does, for sure, and I'd just as soon not tell you the rumors, not yet. But I thought the two families had patched it up long ago. Norris' father, for instance, was the business manager for Martin Howald—Merrill and Abel's father—after Aaron, Jr., left town. And Norris, for a while, was the same for Abel. He would look after the businesses while Abel was busy on some state committee or other."

"I didn't know. Is that why Norris is handling the Howald land now?"

"Probably, although . . ." There was a thoughtful pause, and then Mrs. Strickland went on. "Actually, Norris broke off with Abel, as far as business goes, a couple of years ago. He started up his own real-estate office about that time, and except for this one thing, he hasn't had that much to do with the Howalds or the estate."

"I don't know about Norris and Abel, of course," Sorina supplied, "but there is definitely some mutual antagonism between Norris and Merrill. I don't remember his exact words, but the first time I saw Merrill, he specifically said he had never gotten along well with Norris. In fact, he seemed worried—or annoyed is more like it—that I might have some connection with Norris."

"You? But how could that be?"

"I don't know. Merrill didn't say. He just said—how was it, now? He was afraid Norris had found out about the job the will provided for and had managed to get one of his friends in."

Mrs. Strickland shook her head. "You learn something new every day, I guess. I had no idea that there was still bad blood between the families. Did Merrill say what the trouble was?"

"Not a word. And Amers was pretty good at avoiding the subject, too."

"Odd," Mrs. Strickland said. "People are usually more than happy to talk about their enemies or supposed enemies. But this must be something new. Martin certainly wouldn't have had Norris' father in a responsible position like that if he hadn't liked and trusted him."

"I certainly wouldn't think so. And Abel wouldn't have continued with Norris, either. But you said they had split up a couple of years ago, didn't you? Maybe something got it all started again then."

"I don't think so, but I suppose it's possible. I was under the impression that Norris just wanted to start his own business. The parting was amicable, as far as I know."

"Yes, well, not everything shows up on the surface, apparently," Sorina commented. "Maybe it's just something personal between Merrill and Norris. I think I'll try asking them specifically, now that I know there really was some hostility between the families at one time."

Mrs. Strickland nodded. "Yes, it could be interesting. Maybe they know more than the rumors tell us. But be careful. Don't let yourself get caught in the middle of a family feud."

No, thought Sorina, I mustn't let myself get caught in a family feud. Unfortunately, she had the uncomfortable feeling that she had already been caught.

After supper she called Merrill, but he was out. This time she didn't leave a message. Then, before she had a chance to call Norris Amers, the doorbell rang, and she went to the door to find Amers standing there. He said he had just stopped by to see how she was getting along and if there was anything he could do for her.

"As a matter of fact," Sorina said, thinking of the apparition she had seen in East House the evening before, "there is. Do you have the keys to East House with you?"

He looked puzzled. "I think so, but why?"

"If it's not too much trouble, I'd like to look it over from the inside."

"Yes, well, I don't see why not." He fumbled in his pockets for a few seconds before coming up with a key ring with a dozen keys, all with small pieces of tape attached. "These are the ones, I think."

He looked up at Sorina. "Why the sudden interest in East House? There's really not that much to see. It's almost identical to West House, except the layout of the rooms is reversed. And it hasn't been lived in for fifty years."

Sorina shrugged. "I've always liked to explore, especially houses."

He smiled. "So have I. It's one reason I got into real estate." He paused. "The lights aren't hooked up, by the way."

"That's all right. There's still a little sunlight left. And I have a flashlight if we need one."

"All right, then. You want to go over right now?"

She nodded. "Just as soon as I get a sweater and the flashlight."

She hurried up the stairs and down the hall to her room and was back in a minute, holding the flashlight under one arm as she buttoned the cardigan sweater. Amers, looking a bit bemused at the sudden request for a tour, led the way down the long drive to the other house.

"I've been talking to a few people today," she said as they walked, "some people who knew your father and Abel and Merrill's father."

He glanced down at her, the bemusement still on his face. "Who was that?"

"One of your teachers, for one. Bessie Platte."

"Yes, I remember her. How is she these days? She must be in her eighties."

"Close to ninety, I think. She said she started teaching in 1907."

"I wouldn't be surprised." Norris laughed. "I remember how surprised my father was the first day I came home from school and told him Miss Platte was my teacher. He couldn't believe she was still there after all those years. But how is she? I know she lives just over the hill, so to speak, but I somehow never get around to visiting her. I really should."

"She's fine, considering her age. Very spry and alert."

"Two generations of Amers . . . What did she have to say about us?"

"Not a lot. She just remembered that your father and your uncle were always fighting with the Howald boys."

Some of the smile left his face. "Yes, I suppose they were." He looked down at her as they walked. "What is this, more of your research?"

"As a matter of fact, it probably is. That's why I was talking to Miss Platte, and Art Weaver and a couple of others. I think that's the only way I'm going to get enough material for any kind of history of the Howalds."

"What about those tons of papers and letters that you inherited?"

She shrugged. "There aren't as many as it seemed. The only period that's covered really well is the time that Leroy Howald was in Congress."

"Oh? What about the rest of the time—the other ninety-five percent? All those cabinets and boxes couldn't have been filled with just two terms in Congress."

"Just two filing cabinets. The others, and the boxes, don't have much in them. Merrill thinks maybe Abel never got around to sorting and filing everything. He thought the bulk of the papers might be in one of the offices Abel had around Elston. Handley is supposed to be checking on that now."

"Why would any of those papers be someplace like that?"

"I don't know, unless Abel had some of the office people helping him out with the sorting. You know, something to keep them busy during slack periods—and a way to avoid having to do it all himself."

"It wouldn't surprise me," Amers said, a note of hostility rising in his voice.

"You didn't care much for the Howalds, did you?" she asked bluntly.

Amers' stride faltered for a moment, and he looked down at her. "No, I didn't," he said.

"And your father didn't get along with them very well, either."

A scowl crossed his face, but it was shrugged away. "You sound as if you learned quite a bit from Miss Platte and the others."

"Not a lot, but enough to make me curious about a few things."

"So I see." There was a controlled stiffness in his voice now. "What would you like to know?"

"For instance," Sorina said, plunging ahead, "why at least two generations of Amers have been fighting, if that's the word, with two generations of Howalds."

Amers was silent for a time. "Make that three generations," he said finally, with the air of someone reluctantly revealing something he had been hoping all along to talk about.

"Three?" she nodded, thinking that Mrs. Strickland had been right. "What was it, a political feud?"

Amers shook his head, and his entire face seemed to go rigid. "Nothing that spectacular," he said, his voice as tightly controlled as his face. "Just a little swindling, that's all."

"Yes?" Sorina prompted when Amers again fell silent.

Amers took a deep breath and visibly forced some of the tightness out of his body.

"If you really want to know—and if you really think you want to put something like this into your 'history'—all right. If you do, it'll be the first time we've gotten the truth down on any kind of official paper."

He took another deep breath before going on. "To put it in a nutshell, Leroy and Aaron Howald swindled my grandfather, Simon, out of his share of their partnership."

"Swindled? How?"

"Oh, not an outright swindle, the kind you could put them in jail for. They were too slick for that. It was all legal, or so they say. They just tricked him into selling out to them for practically nothing."

"Tricked him? How?"

"Simple. They made him think they were going broke, and that the land they had was worthless."

"And it turned out to be valuable?"

"You're damned right it did! That was about the time the railroad was coming through this part of the state, and they knew it! They knew when and where, with their political connections!"

"And your grandfather didn't?"

Amers snorted. "If he had, do you think he would have sold out to them the way he did? He got practically nothing!"

Sorina nodded. "I can see how that would make you bitter. But I understood that the last generation—your father and Martin Howald, at least—had made up."

"What gives you that idea?"

"Wasn't your father Martin Howald's business manager? For that matter, weren't you the same, only for Abel instead of Martin?"

Another derisive snort issued from Amers. "That's what you call throwing crumbs to the defeated army. Martin could afford to be generous. It was a good, cheap way to keep his conscience from bothering him about what Leroy and Aaron had done to my grandfather. And Abel, he just carried on the tradition for a while, that's all."

Sorina was silent as they covered the last few steps to the front door of East House.

"I don't suppose," she said finally, "any documentation still exists?"

"Documentation to the swindle? Depends on what you mean by documentation. Something you can use in a court of law, no. If there'd been anything like that . . ."

Amers' voice trailed off, and he was silent as he stood before the door to East House, the keys seemingly forgotten in his hand.

"If there had been anything like that," he went on, his voice a faraway whisper, "you would be writing a history of the Amers family today, not the Howalds."

Abruptly, Amers returned his attention to the set of keys.

"Now," he said, his voice back to normal, "you said you wanted a tour of East House." He located the key he was after and thrust it into the lock. "We'd better hurry if you want to see anything before it gets dark."

Sorina was silent, but she was thinking: Now I'll have to get the other side of the Amers-Howald feud from Merrill. If he knows what the other side is. If his motives, whatever they may be, will allow him to tell me.

Then, as the door swung open, Sorina asked, "Were you here yesterday evening?"

He stopped just inside the door and looked down at her. "You don't remember? I brought you the *Journal* from your mailbox."

"I know. I don't mean that. I mean a little later, about sunset. Were you in East House—this house?"

He shook his head. "This is the first time I've been here in several weeks. Why do you ask?"

She shrugged. "Probably just my imagination. I was walking around the house yesterday about sunset, and I looked in through the library window. I thought I saw someone, just for a second."

"Oh? What did he look like?"

"I couldn't see. It wasn't much more than a shadow. As I said, I'm not sure it wasn't just my imagination. In fact, it probably was. What would anyone be doing here? And how would they get in?"

Amers was frowning now. "I don't know," he said, "but . . . Remember the first night you were here, I said I thought I saw someone outside, around Howald's car?"

She had forgotten, but now she recalled it. "You think it could be the same person?"

"Or the same hallucination. Those things are contagious." He shook his head. "I don't think you should take any chances, though. You ought to call the sheriff."

"Maybe," she said, "but what could he do? Unless your local law enforcement is a lot different than what we have in the cities, the sheriff couldn't do any more than we're doing right now—check the place out."

"You're probably right. Although, since this place is owned by a Howald, they might be able to do a little more." A touch of bitterness edged into his voice as he spoke the last words.

"Let's take a look first," Sorina said. "If we see any evidence that anyone's been here, then we can call."

Amers nodded. "Might as well look at the library first. Isn't that where you say you saw him?"

"If it was a him, not a her, or an it," Sorina muttered, half under her breath.

The living room, as they moved through it slowly, seemed identical to the one in West House, except that, as Amers had said, it was a mirror image. And the furniture, what she could see of it under the dusty sheets, was different. This was the furniture that Aaron Howald, Sr., had used until his death nearly half a century ago. During the brief time Aaron, Jr., had lived here, he had not bothered to change anything, and when he had left, everything had been covered.

In the library the same floor-to-ceiling bookshelves, encased in glass, covered most of the walls. Here, however, at least half of the shelves were empty, and Sorina wondered if Aaron had read less or if the missing books had simply been absorbed into the library in West House. Sorina rather hoped the latter was the case. It would be a shame to let that many books just lie around unused for all those years.

"Where exactly did you see him?" Amers was still standing in the archway between living room and library.

"Just about where you're standing," she said. "A little more in the library."

"Where did he go then?"

"Into the dining room, if he went anywhere."

Amers looked down at the floor, at the ancient, richly flowered carpet that spread through both the library and the living room. The wood floor was bare for about a yard between those two rooms and the dining room, where a dark-green, thick pile carpet covered the floor to within a foot of the walls.

The fading, reddening light that slanted through the library window fell directly on the wall between the living room and the library, with its huge fireplace that opened out into both rooms. The rooms at the back of the house, the dining room and the music room, were in deep shadow.

Sorina switched on her flashlight and shone it down on the uncarpeted section of the floor, then knelt down to look more closely.

"Pretty dusty," she said, "although it hardly looks like a half century of dust."

"It's not," Amers said. "All three houses were cleaned, at least superficially, when they were put on the market."

Sorina leaned down farther, moving from side to side with the flashlight, as if looking for the right direction from which to study the floor.

"Look at this," she said finally. "Do these look like footprints?"

Amers leaned down and looked where she was pointing.

"Possibly," he said, "but I wouldn't guarantee they aren't left over from the last time I showed some people through the place. Still, it might be enough to show the sheriff, if you decide to call him."

"It won't be enough if you tell him *that*—that they could be your own or a potential buyer's footprints. If they're footprints at all."

She stood up. "Come on. Let's look over the rest of the house."

To the surprise of neither of them, they found nothing else that would indicate the presence of anything or anyone other than themselves. They returned to West House by way of the long, dark passageways and the central house, picking their way through the first passage and the central house with Sorina's flashlight.

As they emerged from the kitchen in West House and moved into the dining room, Sorina saw the cat. It was sitting near the edge of the wide door leading to the living room and library, its eyes fixed on them as if it had been waiting, patiently staring at the door to the kitchen until they appeared.

"There," Sorina said, pointing, "there it is."

She started toward it cautiously. "Maybe if I catch it, the two of us can hang onto it long enough to see if there's a name on the collar."

Amers said nothing, but hung back near the kitchen door as Sorina advanced. She leaned down, one hand extended, and talked softly to the cat. At first it sat quietly, its eyes following her as she moved forward. Then, as she came within a couple of feet, its head shifted slightly, dartingly, to one side—as if, Sorina thought, it had suddenly seen a bird. Or a dog.

When she leaned close, the cat's ears lowered and its whole body seemed to tense. Sorina stopped, and she could hear the beginnings of a deep, ominous growl coming from its throat.

"Come on, cat," she said softly, "it's just me. You were friendly enough the other day. What's wrong now?"

Hesitantly, she moved her hand forward another few inches. The guttural growling sound continued, but the animal's eyes were directed somewhere beyond Sorina.

From behind her came Amers' voice. "Looks like it's just me it doesn't like," he said, and Sorina wondered if there was a touch of nervousness in the words.

"But why . . . Have you ever seen it before?"

"No, never, but . . ." His voice trailed away to silence, and Sorina could hear him as he began to move forward. As he did, the cat's eyes moved with him, and the sound it made became even deeper. At the same time, it crouched lower to the floor, the reddish stone in its collar almost vanishing in the fur that ruffed out around its neck.

"Maybe it just doesn't like men," Amers said.

"It sure doesn't care for you, that's for sure." She reached a hand down toward the cat again, murmuring softly, reassuringly.

But it was paying no attention to her. Its eyes were rigidly fixed on Amers as he moved past Sorina slowly, edging well out around the cat.

"You're sure you've never seen it before?"

"Positive," Amers said, and then, after a long pause, he continued in a voice that seemed troubled, distracted. "I have seen a stone like the one in its collar, however."

"Where?" Sorina looked around to him. He was standing half in the library, half in the dining room, his eyes fixed on the cat, even as the cat's were fixed on him.

"Clarice," he said. "Abel's wife. She had one just like it."

"What? You mean this could be her cat after all?"

She glanced back at the cat. "But I was told her cats

had been taken by a sister, one who lives a couple of hundred miles away."

"They were; and this isn't one of her cats anyway. No, it's just the stone, the carnelian . . ."

Suddenly, with an earsplitting yowl that was somehow mixed with a loud hiss, the cat leaped up and darted away through the living room. Behind Sorina, Amers sucked in his breath sharply.

Sorina stared after the cat for a moment before turning to Amers.

"You were saying . . . ?" she prompted. "About the carnelian?"

Amers shook his head and blinked, as if coming out of a trance.

"Carnelian? Oh, yes, the collar." Another blink and a long look in the direction in which the cat had disappeared. "It's probably nothing, just a coincidental resemblance. I was making too much of it."

"But you said this stone looked just like one Clarice Howald owned."

"Yes, quite a bit like it—but I didn't get that close a look at it just now. It was just the color and the shape . . ." He shrugged, and he seemed to be losing the nervousness in his voice. "It probably wouldn't look much like it if I saw it up close."

Sorina thought for a moment. "If it really is that similar, could it be an imitation, made on purpose? Could Mrs. Howald have had one made like that for one of her cats?"

"It's possible, I suppose. But I told you, that wasn't one of her cats."

"I know. But she could have given it to a friend for his or her cat, couldn't she?"

"She could have. But why?"

"Don't ask me," Sorina said. "I'm having trouble imagining anyone making a collar like that for a cat at all, whether it's an imitation or not. At least if it were an imitation of a real stone, it might make a little sense. Not much, but a little. Although I have heard of some pretty weird things people have done for cats. Was Mrs. Howald— Well, a cat nut is the only term, I guess. Was she?"

Amers frowned thoughtfully. "She might have been, although I never thought of it that way before. I didn't know her that well, for one thing. But she did have three cats, and—" He paused as a new thought came to him.

"You know," he went on, "that cat *could* be related to one of hers. She had a long-haired white one, not quite as long-haired as this one, and without most of the markings. And it was a male, I think. I suppose this one could be a son or a cousin or something. As I recall, they weren't always locked up, so . . ."

"You mean Mrs. Howald might have known about it? And had the collar with the imitation carnelian made up as a gift to the cat's owner?"

Amers shrugged. "Why not?" And again there was a touch of bitterness in his tone. "After all, a few dollars—or a few hundred dollars—was nothing to a Howald."

"The cat would have to belong to a neighbor, then," Sorina said, ignoring the tone in Amers' voice. "I already thought it might belong to someone nearby, the way it seems to be commuting between here and wherever its home is. The only questions are, which neighbor is it, and how does the cat get in and out of this house?"

"There aren't that many neighbors, so its owner shouldn't be too hard to locate. As for how it gets in and out—have you checked all the windows?"

"Every one—upstairs, downstairs, and in the basement. Not a crack. And there aren't any special cat doors in any of the regular doors, either."

"None you found, anyway. But if what you say is true, there has to be *some* kind of opening for it to get through."

"I know. I know. Secret panels for cats?"

Amers laughed, but there was not much humor in it.

"Why not? All it would have taken was money." He stopped short of the obvious remark that Sorina half expected to be next.

"Yes," she said lightly, "money does have its advantages, although I have to admit I never would have thought that carnelian cat collars was one of them. Incidentally, there's one way we could get a better idea of how close an imitation it is."

"What's that?" Amers looked down at her, frowning slightly.

"Simple. I got a close look at the collar a day or so ago. I had the cat in my hands, trying to see if there was a name on the collar anywhere."

"So?"

"So, I get someone to show me Mrs. Howald's stone. I could see if they really are almost identical."

Amers shook his head. "I'm afraid not."

"No? Why not? Isn't the stone still here?"

An odd, humorless smile played on Amers' lips. "Oh, it's still here, but I doubt that you could see it, not without a great deal of trouble."

"And why is that?" Sorina asked sharply, beginning to be annoyed.

"Very simple. The stone was in a necklace—a choker, to be exact—and Clarice Howald is still wearing it. In her coffin."

8

Sorina was silent for several seconds. "Oh," she said finally. "But there must be pictures of it somewhere."

"Not that I know of," Amers said. "Although if you wanted to you could probably talk to the jeweler she bought it from."

"She bought it in Elston?"

"I don't know. I would rather doubt it, though."

"And you don't have any idea where she did buy it? Or where she might have gotten a copy made?"

"None," he said, shaking his head in mock sadness. "I'm afraid I don't travel in the same circles that the Howalds did."

Sorina frowned as she looked up at him, directly into his eyes. "Does *everything* we talk about eventually lead to a put-down of the Howalds because of their money?"

He seemed taken aback for a moment, but he recovered quickly and shrugged. "Not quite, but a great many things do. You'll have to excuse me, but it's a hard habit to break after all these years."

"If you feel that strongly, why are you handling these houses?"

"Why not? It does give me a certain amount of control over them—him. A small amount, admittedly, but an amount nonetheless. Besides, one does not turn down the possibility of several thousand dollars in commissions unless he is either independently wealthy or stupid. On my good days, at least, I am neither."

"I'm sure you're not," she said, adding, "but when was your last good day?"

She paused a second before going on. "And before

you can get all up in arms about that remark, I'll apologize. You left such an opening, it was hard to resist showing you how easy it is to make cheapshot put-downs. Like about Howald money."

Amers had stiffened but now seemed to relax a little, a faint smile pulling at his lips. "I see what you mean. I hereby declare a moratorium on put-downs of Howald money. Is that what you want?"

"It'll do," she said, wondering why she seemed to be continually defending the Howalds, against Merrill Howald himself and now against Norris Amers. "In the meantime, you still don't have any idea where Clarice might have gotten the necklace? Or the possible imitation?"

"Not a one. All I can suggest is that you ask Merrill. Or check with all the jewelers in Elston. There aren't very many."

"I imagine not. But I'll try asking Merrill first. Although, come to think of it, I already told him about it, even described it to him, and we looked up the type of stone at the library. All of that, and he didn't say anything about Clarice owning a necklace like that."

"Maybe he never saw it," Amers suggested. "Don't forget, he hasn't been here except for occasional visits for over ten years."

"But he must have seen it at the funeral."

"Perhaps, but would he remember it? Would you?"

"Maybe not."

They had continued to walk slowly through the house as they talked, and now, as they neared the front door, Amers stopped to look down at her earnestly.

"You've decided not to call the sheriff about the possible prowler?" he asked, shifting back to their earlier discussion without warning.

"I think so," she said. "Unless it gets worse, there's not much he could do. And I'm still not sure that I believe in the prowler's existence. A couple of shadows and a face in the window aren't enough."

Amers was silent for several seconds before he spoke again. "Would you like a gun?" he asked finally.

"A gun? For what?"

"In case your prowler is really real and in case you need a gun. I have an extra pistol you can have if you want it. It's only a target twenty-two, but it should do the job. All you have to do is show it."

"Sure, and then it gets taken away from me. I don't think so, not right now. Maybe later."

He shrugged. "All right. It's your prowler. And your neck, so to speak." He glanced at his watch. "And I have to be going now. Another house to show this evening."

With a final "Be careful," he was gone.

Sorina awoke with the feeling that she was being watched, and as she moved her eyes around the room, she saw that she was—just as she had been the night before and the night before that. In the near total darkness a trio of dimly glowing, red-tinged eyes peered up at her from the floor a few feet from the bed, and Sorina couldn't help but wonder if the cat's eyes and the carnelian in its collar were battery operated. Cat's eyes and jewels are theoretically visible only through reflected light, and inside a house, on a night when only the faintest wisp of moonlight filtered through a thin layer of clouds, there should have been no light that they could reflect.

And yet they glowed.

Sorina could not repress a shiver as the image of another carnelian, glowing softly in the blackness of a coffin, floated eerily through her mind.

More rapidly than she had intended, her hand shot out to fumble for the bedside lamp. The image faded and the prickle of gooseflesh that had come with the image retreated as the shadows were pressed backward to the corners of the room and into the hall beyond the door.

For a full minute Sorina lay, leaning on one elbow,

watching the cat, wondering. How *did* it get in and out so easily? Could there actually be, as Norris had sarcastically suggested, a secret panel for a cat? A brief smile tugged at her lips as the thought crossed her mind.

A more important question, though, might be *why* the cat kept returning here.

She shook her head and sat up, throwing the covers back.

"Come on, cat, whoever or whatever you are," she said, grabbing up the terrycloth robe from the bed and pushing her feet into her slippers, "let's get this over with. You let me catch you, and I find out who you belong to, okay?"

The cat, its eyes alert and seemingly riveted on Sorina, moved toward the door to the hall as soon as she stood up and knotted the belt of her robe.

"Look, cat," Sorina muttered as she grabbed the flashlight from the bedside table, "who do you think you are? Lassie? Are you trying to lead me someplace? Or do you just like to have people follow you around?"

As if in answer, the cat trotted into the hall, carefully staying out of Sorina's reach, carefully keeping a watch on her as it moved.

Sorina sighed. "All right, cat, if that's the way it's going to be . . ."

She followed it down the hall toward the stairs. "You're not getting away this time, not until I see how you pull your vanishing act. No distractions, just you and me. And if I can't keep track of you, you've had it. Next time I close and latch the bedroom door, so you just be warned and act accordingly."

The cat, stopping every three or four steps to look back, trotted down the stairs. At the bottom it turned to the left, toward the living room and the library end of the house. Sorina, remembering how it had somehow managed to get not only into the kitchen but through the kitchen into the connecting passageway the other night, hurried after it. She didn't pause to search out the light switches, but flipped on the flashlight and fixed its beam on the retreating animal.

And this time, it didn't vanish. Instead, it sat waiting at the door to the kitchen. Keeping the flashlight carefully trained on the animal, Sorina turned on the dining-room lights and then advanced. The cat sat perfectly still except for its eyes, which looked back and forth between the door to the kitchen and Sorina.

Cautiously, keeping up what she hoped was a soothing line of cat patter, Sorina stooped down, touched the cat lightly on the head, then stroked it tentatively. It continued to look first at Sorina, then at the door, and back again.

"What happened, cat? Did you lose your touch? Your secret escape hatch blocked?"

Still moving slowly, talking to the animal softly, Sorina picked it up. When it did not protest except for a momentary struggle toward the door, she moved back to the sheet-draped table directly under the chandelier.

"Okay, let's see that collar; okay, cat?" As she set the animal on the table, it mewed once, softly, and its eyes looked into Sorina's. They were large and expressive, and of an odd reddish shade that almost matched the stone around its neck. But underneath . . .

Sorina squinted and looked more closely. Mixed with the red, almost like a background, was a faint gray-green.

But the eyes weren't what she was interested in, she told herself, it was the collar. And that was where the trouble started the time before, she thought, when she had tried to take the collar off.

Continuing her soothing monologue, Sorina put her fingers on the collar. Definitely velvet, or a damned good imitation, she thought as she ran her fingers around it, first on the outside, then on the inside.

Then the stone. She looked at it closely for several seconds, wondering if it could be a catch of some kind, if the collar was made like one of those "take-it-apart-in-less-than-an-hour-and-you're-a-genius" puzzles. It would, she supposed, preclude the cat from getting the collar off by itself, but it certainly wouldn't keep anyone who wanted to steal the stone from simply cutting the collar off—if he could catch the cat, of course.

Cautiously, Sorina twisted at the stone, pushed at it, pulled at it, and did everything else she could think of to it—but nothing happened. Finally she turned the collar out a section at a time so that she could get a look at its underside.

But there was nothing—nothing that she could find, at any rate.

"All right, cat, I give up. Whatever the secret of your collar is, it's safe from me. What now? You want to go back to your imitation of Lassie?"

And me? she wondered. I'll go back to my imitation of a wacky old lady following a cat around an old house, talking to herself all the way.

As if on cue, the cat leaped to the floor and promptly returned to its post by the kitchen door. Food? Sorina wondered. Was that why it was heading to the kitchen door this time instead of vanishing? It could vanish only on a full stomach?

She pushed open the door, and the cat darted through. Apparently it wasn't hungry, for it shot straight across the floor and was sitting waiting at the door to the passageway almost before Sorina was all the way into the kitchen.

"So it's the Lassie imitation again, is it? Okay, cat, I've made this much of a fool of myself already, there's no reason not to go all the way. But unless you can vanish again, you're not getting much farther. I don't have a key to the other end of this thing. And if a ghost or anything pops out, you do the honors, okay?"

The cat mewed once, softly, as Sorina pulled the door open, and immediately darted through and pelted down the curving steps. At the bottom it stopped and looked back up.

"How about the garage, cat? You want in there?" But the cat hurried past the garage door without a glance, and in a few seconds it was sitting at the far end of the passageway, at the door to the central house.

"No luck, cat. You weren't listening, were you? I told you I don't have the key to that door. Now if you were really as smart as Lassie, you'd know what I was talking about. You wouldn't waste all our time this way, right?"

She reached for the knob. "See, cat, it doesn't turn; it's—"

But it did turn.

Sorina fell silent, and a sudden chill spread over her despite the warm terrycloth robe that was wrapped tightly about her.

Norris, she thought; he forgot to lock this when we came through here this evening. That's all.

She pushed the door open and let it swing back. The cat darted through immediately and sat waiting a few feet beyond. Here, as at the other end of the passageway, was a kitchen, only it was smaller and much more crowded, because the center of the room was taken up by a table large enough for all the servants who had once worked in both houses to eat at. She stood for a moment in the doorway, playing the beam of the flashlight around the room and onto the door on the far side, which opened, she knew, on a narrow hallway. Beyond that was a fairly large sitting room, presumably where the servants could gather for whatever group recreations they went in for.

Looking down, she saw the cat waiting for her by the door to the hall. No longer bothering to question her actions or wonder why the hell she continued in this insane follow-the-leader game with a cat, she crossed the kitchen and pushed the door open. The cat darted through and immediately took up an expectant post at the back door, at the end of the narrow hall.

"You're taking me outside, is that it, cat? Then why did you lead me through that— Oh, never mind. The way things are going, either you're going to answer me or I'm going to start thinking that you really should.

And this damned door, which has probably been locked for years, will just be conveniently open, right?"

She reached for the knob, hesitating at the last second, afraid that she would be right, and afraid that, if she were, she would not be able to find a rational explanation.

But it was only for an instant, and then she was turning the knob and pulling the door open. All right, she told herself as the door swung open, now is the time for common sense to prevail. Now is the time for me to let the cat out and go back to bed. Now is the time . . .

But she didn't, and in the few seconds she hesitated, the cat had pushed open the screen door with its head and was slipping away into the darkness. With no more hesitation, Sorina shoved the screen door open and followed, the beam of the flashlight showing the cat a half dozen yards out, just to one side of the rickety-looking shed. In the faint beam of the flashlight, the shed seemed to be leaning, and the door, next to which the cat was sitting, was hanging partially open.

Sorina started toward the cat, glancing down once to see if the grass was wet, thinking: If I'd known I was going on another tour of the estate, I'd have taken time to put my shoes on.

But the grass was relatively dry and not overly tall here, so it wasn't too bad. Passing the shed, she flashed the beam over the wide crack along one side of the door. Toolshed, she seemed to remember, and that other building off to the right, somewhat bigger and not quite so dilapidated, was the smokehouse.

In the meantime the cat was beyond the toolshed and almost beyond the range of the light, heading back toward— Toward what? The stables? The gazebo behind East House? Or the orchard, perhaps? That's where she had seen it the day before, crossing the small bridge into the orchard.

"That's as far as I go, cat—the bridge. If you want me any farther, you'll have to wait until I go back for some shoes. All right? And maybe for some daylight, too. We can't go wandering over the entire countryside in the middle of the night. At least I can't, I don't know about you."

But the cat was forging ahead, staying just in range of the flashlight's weakening beam. "And that's something else, cat. If you keep this up, I'll need new batteries—and I'm not wandering around in the dark, not even for a feline imitation of Lassie. Understand?"

But the cat moved on, stopping every few feet to look back over its shoulder at Sorina. And judging from the direction it was taking, generally toward the northeast, past the oval of the horse track, it was indeed heading once again for the orchard. About halfway there, Sorina stopped. A few feet farther on the cat stopped and again looked back at her. Its soft mewing was almost lost in the open air and the light breeze that came from the south, around the houses.

"Sorry, cat; I warned you."

Sorina stood for a minute, the flashlight pointed along the ground ahead. Fifty yards away she could just make out the shadowy shapes of the trees and the pale spot that was the bridge across the twisting creek, and for an instant she thought she could see movement, a darker shadow among the other shadows.

But it was nothing. No one would be wandering through the orchard in the dark, in the middle of the night. That would be just as unlikely as someone wandering around the rest of the grounds in a ratty robe and slippers, carrying a failing flashlight, following an insistent cat . . .

Before she could succumb to further foolishness, Sorina turned sharply back toward the houses.

And stopped.

She flipped off the flashlight and stood motionless, her eyes straining.

A light, faint and uncertain, but a light—in one of the windows of East House. The house that had lain deserted and unused for half a century.

The shadowy form she had seen in the library of

East House, the face she had glimpsed through the glass of the back door, the seemingly sourceless moans —all came crowding back into her mind in an instant. And now a light where there should be no light . . .

This, she thought, should certainly be enough to get the sheriff out here. *If* it's not just Amers again, checking things out. If . . .

The flashlight still off, she started toward the spot of light.

Careful, she told herself as she walked, careful. No noise. Don't fall over your own feet. Just take a quick look in the window, then get the hell out of there and make that call to the sheriff's office. That's all, just a quick look so that if whoever it is has vanished by the time the sheriff gets here, I'll be able to tell him who it was or what he looked like.

From the location of the light, it must be in the dining room, she thought, trying to picture the layout of the rooms. Yes, the dining room. She veered to the right, aiming now toward the passageway that connected East House with the central building. It seemed safer to approach the dining-room windows in that roundabout way rather than directly.

In a minute she was at the corner of the house, the kitchen windows dimly visible above her. She hesitated briefly, once again doubting her sanity, but then pushed ahead, keeping close to the wall as she moved.

She stopped just before reaching the first dining-room window. She listened, but could hear nothing but the faint whisper of the breeze through the hedges and trees a dozen yards away.

Now or never, she thought, and moved the last few inches and peered through the corner of the window. The light, she saw, was coming from a shaded flashlight. It was set on the dining-room table, next to something that looked like a box. And to one side, his back to the window, was a man. Only one arm and a shoulder were visible, and there was no way of telling who it was.

Then from the part of the room beyond her view, another man appeared, moving toward the light and the box on the table. He was a large man, broad as well as tall, obviously neither Norris Amers nor Merrill Howald.

Then who . . . ?

If only he would turn to face this way, just for a moment. His hair, she noticed as he moved away from the window toward the table, was light, probably gray rather than blond, and seemed to be combed straight back. And he was wearing dark pants and shirt, possibly gray also, though the light was not bright enough for her to distinguish colors readily.

He turned, and Sorina stifled a gasp as she recognized the face.

The face that she had seen for the first time only that afternoon—on a poster at the Portman County State Prison Farm.

The face of William Barlow!

9

William Barlow! Had he been here all this time? Had he stayed here, hidden in this house for the entire year since he had killed the Howalds?

Sorina's heart was pounding as she moved back from the window, holding her breath in an effort to be utterly silent, and she wondered if this could possibly be anything but a bad dream, a nightmare. Things like this just didn't happen, not to real people.

But then the chilling thought came to her: Entire families don't get themselves murdered for no reason, either . . .

From somewhere came the yowl of a cat, an eerie, piercing shriek that froze every muscle in Sorina's body, and she was thinking:

Not now, damn it! *Not now!*

Before she could do more than think, the face of William Barlow appeared at the window, still only yards away. In the dim light she could see a frown crossing his face, and his arm motioning to the other man in the room.

She turned and ran, worrying no more about being silent, worrying only about reaching safety.

But where? Where would she be safe? Not the house, certainly. They could break the doors down easily enough, or come through a window.

The car? But she didn't have her keys with her!

Behind her she heard a door thrown open and footsteps pounding across the ground.

Damn these short legs! she thought, regretting her diminutive frame for the first—and possibly the last—time in her life. She forced herself to move even faster, to ignore the slipper that had flopped loose and threatened to fly off, to ignore everything but the door of the central house, which she could now see dimly ahead of her in the faint beam of the flashlight.

On her right the toolshed loomed up, and for an instant she considered dodging in there, grabbing up whatever weapon she could find, and turning to face her pursuers. But she wasn't sure she could get the door open fast enough or that there was anything in there that would do her any good. No, her best bet was to reach the door of the central house and go through to the connecting passageway. The other doors to West House were locked, and that should give her enough time to phone the sheriff and barricade herself in her room on the second floor.

But *were* the doors locked? The question jolted through her: She had thought the doors to the central house were locked, too.

But at least she could lock the kitchen door behind her. There was, she remembered, a bolt that could be thrown, so if she could just reach the kitchen of West House . . .

And by the door of the dining room, she suddenly remembered, were those heavy, ornamental candlesticks. She could grab one of those on the run. It might not be much, but it was something.

If only she could make it to the back door of the central house!

Then the door was within her grasp, and she flung it open, hearing the footsteps closing in behind her. She leaped through, slammed the door after her, and ran blindly toward the door to the kitchen and—

—into the outstretched arms of Merrill Howald!

She screamed once, involuntarily, and kicked frantically. She landed one glancing blow on his shin.

Then he had her firmly by both shoulders, literally holding her out at arms' length as she thrashed about, her feet barely touching the floor. The flashlight was somewhere on the floor, casting wildly shifting shadows as it rolled.

"It's all right, Sorina!"

It was Merrill's rumbling bass, practically shouting in her face. "We're not going to hurt you! Do you understand?"

For an instant the words did not register.

"Barlow—" she began, but Merrill cut her off.

"That's right, Barlow. *James* Barlow! William's brother."

Behind her she could hear the door opening and footsteps approaching. Abruptly, she relaxed in Merrill's grip, going almost totally limp. Her arms and legs suddenly felt as if they were made of rubber, and it was only Merrill's hands on her arms that kept her from falling.

"Are you all right now?" he asked, loosening his grip slightly. "Will you stay put while we explain things to you?"

The other man, Barlow, came into her line of sight and leaned over to pick up the flashlight. After a brief glance at Merrill, he held the light out to Sorina.

Slowly, as Merrill released his grip on her arms, she reached out and took the light. From some deeply implanted reflex came the words, "Thank you," as she took the light into her hand.

Merrill looked down at her feet for a moment, then back at Barlow. "Jim, why don't you check outside for her missing slipper?"

Barlow nodded once and left.

"Let's go back to West House; you'll be more comfortable there."

Again he glanced down at her one bare foot, and a slight grin became evident behind the close-cropped beard. "Come on, just relax, and I'll carry you to the nearest rug. It's the least I can do after making you lose your slipper and practically fracture my shin."

She tensed for a moment, then relaxed once more. If they had been planning to do anything drastic to her, they would have done it already.

"All right," she said, and then, as he picked her up

easily and pushed through the door to the kitchen and across to the passageway door, "you did say you had a rational explanation for this whole affair, didn't you?"

His laugh, almost as deep as his voice, boomed out practically in her ear.

"An explanation, yes," he said as he moved down the steps into the passageway, "but I'll leave it to you whether it's rational or not. At this point I'm beginning to have doubts myself—more doubts than I had before, that is."

She felt her heart slowing from the horrendous pounding of the last few minutes to a mere thumping. And she couldn't help but notice, even now, the total effortlessness with which he seemed to carry her. There must be more strength in those arms than his lean frame would indicate.

"And that explanation is . . . ?" she asked as they neared the steps leading up to the kitchen of West House.

He was silent as they went up the steps and into the kitchen. He kicked the door shut behind them and continued through the kitchen and into the dining room, where he put her down. The thick rug felt soft and warm under her bare foot. Merrill walked on into the living room, touching something on the wall near the light switch as he went. He grabbed the sheets on a couple of the chairs and yanked them off in small clouds of dust.

"We can wait here till Jim gets back," he said. "In the meantime, I don't suppose you would reconsider my earlier offer? To take a nice, lucrative, and satisfying job somewhere else in the country?"

She shook her head. "After what just happened out there?" she asked incredulously.

Merrill Howald sighed. "Somehow I didn't think you would. All right, you might as well sit down. This may take a while. I'm not sure where to start."

"At the beginning? Or is that being naïve?"

"If there *was* a beginning . . ." He shook his head

and sat down as Sorina herself collapsed into one of the chairs and tucked her bare foot under her. "If there was one, I suppose it was when Abel and his family were killed last year. Theoretically by William Barlow, escaped convict."

"From your tone—and from the fact that you have his brother here with you—I gather you don't think he did it."

"Quite right. To start with, there are no reasons why he should have. And a dozen reasons why he shouldn't—couldn't—have. It just doesn't make sense for him to have done it."

Sorina nodded. "I heard a few of those reasons this afternoon, from Warden Ormand."

"You were at the prison farm, then?"

"For a while," she said. "That's where I saw Barlow's picture."

"Yes, well, Jim does look quite a bit like Bill—William. And if all you've seen is that poster . . . But if you've been talking to Ormand, at least you'll know what I'm talking about. Barlow was a trustee, for one thing. He was using a prison car, which he is supposed to have left sitting in the middle of Elston—not hidden somewhere so he would have some extra time before they found it, but right out in the open, where someone was sure to see it. Everybody in town recognizes the prison cars. For another, he had only a few months of his sentence left to serve. He had no reason to escape, not for that short a time. And he had no reason to come here, to Abel's place. And even assuming he did come here, he had no reason at all to kill anyone."

"Yes, Ormand said about the same thing. He also said he suspected Barlow didn't really escape, but that he was kidnaped. Possibly by the brothers of the man he was in prison for killing."

"I know that's one of the theories, but I doubt it."

"What, then?"

Merrill glanced down at the floor, hesitating. "I think

he was kidnaped all right," he said finally, speaking slowly, "but I think the kidnaper was someone else."

Again he hesitated, as if doubtful, even now, that he should go on.

"Yes? Who do you think it was?" Sorina prompted after several seconds of silence.

Merrill leaned forward in his chair, turning slightly so that his eyes met hers directly.

"Norris Amers," he said quietly.

She blinked once, murmuring the name softly to herself. Norris Amers. She couldn't say why, but she was not surprised, not really. Had she suspected something like that herself? Or was it just that, after her terror-stricken dash of only a few minutes ago, she was temporarily out of emotions?

"You don't seem overly surprised," Merrill was saying.

She shook her head. "I suppose I should be, but . . . Maybe I will be later. In any event, why do you think it was Amers? Certainly not just the feud, or whatever it is, that your families seem to have been carrying on for the past three generations."

"So you heard about that, did you? From Amers? If so, it must have been a pretty one-sided account."

"From him, yes, but I heard a little about it from one of the neighbors first. Bessie Platte. She taught two generations of Howalds and Amers, and she remembers they spent a lot of time fighting."

"Did she say why? Or did Norris?"

"She didn't know. And Norris said your grandfather and Aaron Howald cheated his grandfather out of his share of the business. I meant to ask you about that the next time I saw you."

Merrill sighed. "Unfortunately, he *may* be right. To be completely fair, it all depends on whether you believe my ancestors or his. I've never decided for sure myself."

"I've heard the Amers version. What's the Howald version?"

"And the Amers version is what? That Leroy and Aaron lied to old Simon Amers about the value of the land, while they knew secretly that the railroad was going to make the land skyrocket in value?"

"That's about it. It sounds nasty enough, and plausible."

"I know. As I said, it *may* have happened that way. The other version is that Simon Amers was taking more out of the business than he was putting in—some book juggling, that sort of thing—and got caught. Rather than have him arrested, they agreed to 'buy him out,' at a price that took into account at least some of what he'd stolen, and let the whole thing slide, in hopes that it could all be kept quiet."

"What about the books he juggled?" Sorina asked. "Couldn't someone look at those and see who's telling the truth?"

"If they still existed, yes, but they don't. They were all destroyed in a fire not long after the partnership was 'dissolved.' Arson was suspected, but no one was ever able to prove anything. So either side could have done it to destroy the evidence. Or it could have all been an accident, a coincidence."

"So no one will ever know for sure?"

"Probably not. Unless there really *are* some old papers of my grandfather's that would shed some light on the subject. I doubt it, though. If there were, they would've been found by now."

"And the reason for Norris' father working for yours?"

"Probably roughly the same reason Norris gave you. My father didn't think Harold Amers should have to suffer for what Simon did, if he really did do anything. Besides, Harold Amers was a damn good manager, from what I've heard."

"And Norris?"

"I don't know, and now we're getting to the reason we're here."

"I was wondering about that. What *is* the reason you

two were lurking about in the other house? And, incidentally, was Barlow the one I saw in the library of East House yesterday? And outside the back door of this one last night?"

Merrill nodded. "And it was him that Norris got a glimpse of that first night you were here. As for what we're doing here, maybe I *had* better try to start from the beginning. Or maybe I should just let you read this as a start."

He reached into a jacket pocket and pulled out a folded piece of paper and handed it across to her.

"Just the last paragraph," he said, "that's the important part. It's the last letter I got from Abel, a couple of months before he was killed."

Sorina took the paper, unfolded it, and turned it so that it caught the light from the dim fixture overhead. The letter was typed, and it seemed to have been written not long after the one she remembered seeing in the files, the one in which Merrill had denied any interest in returning to Elston. In the last paragraph, Abel Howald said:

> You may be right, though, in wanting to steer clear of Elston and everything that goes with it. There are times I don't think anything changes from one century to the next. And if you're wondering what wrung this piece of unsought philosophy from me, it's Norris Amers. You remember I told you that he quit working for the family several months ago and started dealing in real estate. Well, I've been going over our books lately, and I'm beginning to suspect where he got the money to set up shop. Sound familiar? I hope to hell I'm wrong, but . . . Keep your fingers crossed that history doesn't decide to repeat itself.

Sorina looked up from the letter. "And you think Norris could have killed your brother—and his whole family—because he was caught embezzling some money? Doesn't that sound a bit drastic?"

"Stranger things have happened. Isn't that the way the cliché goes?"

"Is that letter all the evidence you have?"

"The only direct evidence, I'm afraid. That's one reason I didn't do anything about it until recently. Abel didn't write any more letters, probably because I never answered *that* one. But not long ago, I tried to check out the books he was talking about. There are some missing, and no one has any idea where they could have gotten to."

"I see what you mean," Sorina admitted. "Still, from embezzlement to mass murder is a big step."

"Admittedly. And it's taken me almost a year to make the step. A year—and Jim Barlow."

"Yes, that's something else I was wondering about. How does Barlow fit into this?"

"As you might imagine, he never did believe his brother killed Abel—and he knew of a few reasons no one else did, including a couple of letters from Bill, letters making plans for when he would be released in just a few months. He contacted me a few months ago, asking the usual questions, the same ones the police asked a year ago. Did Abel have any enemies, etcetera. To make a long story short, we convinced each other that there was a good chance that Norris did it and framed Bill Barlow. Jim hadn't known about Amers and the possible embezzlement. I hadn't really given any thought to anyone other than Bill Barlow being the killer. As you say, it's a long step from embezzlement to mass murder, and I was more than willing to go along with the popular story, that an escaped convict had gone berserk and done them all in. I'm still not one hundred percent sure that Norris did it, but I'm sure enough to spend some time to push it a lot further."

"All right," Sorina said, "but what were you doing out here in the middle of the night? How does lurking around here prove anything about Norris Amers?"

"As they say in the cheap detective movies, it's all part of an elaborate—and possibly useless, certainly impractical—plan. A plan that, I should add, you have been fouling up entirely."

"Me? How? And just what is this elaborate plan? I might as well know what it is I've been wrecking."

"Mostly it revolves around the phony will, setting up the fund for the family history."

"Phony will? You mean Abel didn't—"

"No, he didn't. That was a scheme cooked up by Barlow and myself and Ed Handley, the estate lawyer. The plan was to get Barlow's sister—who doesn't look like either of the brothers, and has never been seen by Amers—to do the 'history.' That's why we stuck in all the restrictions about who could be hired for the job—someone from out of the county, who couldn't possibly be influenced by the local Howald reputation. If we hadn't, the Society could've hired anyone. The idea was, we would put an ad in some faraway paper, and Barlow's sister, Kathy, would show up and apply for the job. If necessary, Handley or I would put in an appearance to make sure she got it."

He shook his head. "But then, before we could even get the ad placed, *you* showed up out of nowhere. And before we knew what was happening, you had gotten the job and moved into the house. The first I knew anything about it was when I saw a light in the house that night and came in to investigate. Jim Barlow was with me, but he stayed outside, which is when Amers got a glimpse of him. Luckily he didn't see him close enough to recognize him."

"I'm sorry I was so prompt," Sorina said. "But I still don't see what your 'plan' is. What does doing a family history have to do with anything?"

"Nothing, directly. It's just an excuse to have someone in the house, officially, to appear to go through all the papers and correspondence. The idea was that after a couple of weeks Kathy would stumble across a copy of one of Abel's letters, a lot like the real one I just showed you, only more positive in its accusations. And other notes also would be found, making references to the missing books and all that."

"All phony?" Sorina frowned. "What good would that do?"

"Maybe none, but Kathy was then going to take the letters and confront Amers with them, and threaten to blackmail him."

"The light comes at last. She might jolt him into doing something rash that would give himself away. But do you think that sort of thing would work in real life? And what about the danger to your imitation blackmailer?"

"I have no idea whether it would work or not, but nobody had any better ideas, not at the time. We were just going to play it by ear. As for the danger, Kathy was more than willing to take the risk, and Jim was going to be keeping a damned close watch on her. There are lots of places in this house that you can hide in. She would never have been alone while Amers was around. In fact, we were hoping he *would* try something. It would be proof of a sort."

"And after that? If it worked out that way?"

"I'm not sure. We'd have everything recorded, of course, but . . . We were thinking about a little haunting, even. Maybe trying to confront him with the victims' spirits in hopes that would jar something loose. Amers *is* somewhat superstitious, I've found out, so who knows? Maybe it would work. Although," he went on with a sudden grin, "it didn't with you."

"The moans last night?"

"That's right. It's part of the intercom system. There are speakers hidden all over the house. Jim was keeping an eye on you through the window, just to see how it worked. He didn't expect you to see him, and he certainly didn't expect you to come charging out after him even if you did. It was lucky the door had that double lock and you didn't have your keys. Anyway, he was in favor of explaining things to you then, but . . . Anyway, that's what we were doing in East House just now, trying to figure out how he could scare you out, wondering if there was any way to hide that projector we had, wondering if it was even possible to scare you out. For a ghost to be effective, the person being haunted can't come charging straight at it the way you apparently do."

"And the cat?" Sorina asked. "Is that part of your haunting, too?"

Merrill's face clouded at the mention. "No, it's not. It's another reason I thought you might have been tied in with Amers somehow. The collar—"

"I know. Amers told me. The stone, the carnelian, is pretty much a duplicate of one in a necklace that Clarice wore. We were trying to figure out where it could have come from."

"You're sure about that collar? You weren't just imagining it?"

"Hardly. I was looking at—" She stopped as the memory of what she had been doing out in the yard came back. "I was looking at it very closely just a short while ago," she went on, "just before I ran into you two. This time, though, after I let the cat go, it didn't just vanish. It kept going to doors and— Well, I thought at the time it was doing a damned good imitation of Lassie. I swear it was trying to lead me someplace. It was headed into the orchard when I decided I'd had enough and turned around to come back. That's when I saw your light in the other house. Incidentally, now that we're laying all our cards on the table, *is* there any way that cat can get in and out of the house by itself?"

He shook his head. "Not that I know of."

"There has to be *someplace*. Unless there are two cats with carnelian collars."

"It's hard enough to imagine one," he said, "let alone two. I suppose there might be someplace, though. Did you check all the windows? Maybe one is open a couple of inches. It doesn't take much for a cat to wriggle through."

"I checked them all, from the basement to the second floor, and there's not a crack. And that reminds me of something else I was planning to ask you. Since the stone in the collar is apparently almost a duplicate of the one in Clarice's necklace, is it possible that she herself had it made for someone? As a gift?"

"Possible, but for whom? And why?"

"Those were my next questions. Norris said the cat resembled one that Clarice had, though it obviously wasn't the same cat. A son or daughter, maybe. He said Clarice's cats spent much of their time outside, so anything's possible. If something like that happened, and Clarice found out about it . . ."

He shrugged. "I didn't know her well enough to say it's impossible, but I can't see her doing anything like that. It's probably just a coincidence. Cats are being dumped or running away all the time. I remember there was a new cat or two every year when I was a kid here."

"But the collar—"

"I know, it's too valuable to throw away with the cat, and if the cat had run away, there would be somebody looking for it. All I can say is, people do very strange things sometimes. Don't forget why we're here—a mass murder. And whoever did it—Norris Amers or Bill Barlow or someone else—certainly wasn't rational."

Suddenly she was sad, and she wondered why the feeling was hitting her now instead of several minutes before, when the deaths of Abel and his family had first been mentioned. Were her emotions only now recovering from the earlier shock?

"I'm sorry," she said. "You're probably right." She pulled in a breath in a half sigh. "Now, just what do you want me to do? Shall I tell the Society that I can't take the job after all? I've already told them about the missing papers, and that the project may fall through if they aren't found."

He shook his head. "Now that we've gone this far, I think you should stay. If you're willing to stay, of course. Would you be willing to go through with what we were planning originally for Kathy?"

As he spoke, Sorina felt relief seeping through her, without knowing precisely why she should feel relieved. Certainly the thought of leaving Elston would not disturb her. Or the thought of not seeing Merrill anymore.

Or would it? Her mind darted back to the evening before, and the feel of his lips on hers. And the sadness she had felt only moments ago, which she realized now must be the result of the empathy she felt with Merrill.

"Your leaving at this stage," he went on, "and our bringing Kathy in to replace you might make Amers suspicious. And he's probably a little suspicious already if you told him about the missing papers. *Did* you tell him, by the way?"

She nodded. "I mentioned that they were pretty skimpy, but he seemed to accept the explanation that they might be in one of Abel's offices."

"He's probably still wondering, though. Anyway, Jim and I were talking about that this evening, wondering if there was a way of getting you out without arousing suspicion. That and ways to bribe or scare you off, although we had just about given up on that. Of course, if you *want* to leave . . ."

"Now that I'm this far in?" she heard herself saying. "I could hardly leave now."

As the words emerged, she wondered: Why?

But she spent little time on speculation. It was enough that she was aware of the fact that she was not being strictly logical or sensible and that she was letting herself in for more problems than she really wanted—just as she had not been overwhelmingly logical that time, four years ago, when she had struck out on her own. Logical or not, it had been something she had wanted to do, had felt that she had to do. And now, in some odd way, it was the same, a strange combination of curiosity and stubbornness—and, she added to herself as her eyes met Merrill's, a certain amount of involvement.

She looked around as she heard a noise from the kitchen. She tensed for a moment, and then relaxed as the door to the kitchen swung open and Jim Barlow came though, holding a damp, bedraggled-looking slipper in one hand.

"Norris?"

"Who—Sorina? Is that you?" Norris Amers' voice on the telephone was still thick with sleep. "What time is it?"

"About midnight. I'm sorry to wake you up, but I've come across something I think you should know about."

"What? What are you—"

Abruptly he was silent, and when he spoke again, all the sleep was gone from his voice. "What is it, Sorina?"

"Something I've found—in these papers I've been going through. You'd better come over."

"Now? Can't it wait until morning?" The voice sounded as if he already knew the answer to the question.

"It could, but . . . I think you'll want to see it as soon as possible."

A momentary pause, then, "All right. Ten minutes."

She hung up, leaning back in the swivel chair by the desk. After she had agreed to take part in his plan, Merrill spent the next two days coaching her in what she had to do. Now the bait was cast. In ten minutes the game would be in full swing, and there would be no backing out.

She looked again at the letter, typed roughly and, of course, not signed. It followed much the same lines as the actual letter that Merrill had received, except Abel's suspicions were played up more. The important paragraph now began, "I probably shouldn't say anything about this until I have definite proof, but . . ." The letter continued for another paragraph, and then stopped in midsentence, as if it had been abandoned and not picked up again. It was meant to look as if Abel had told no one of his suspicions outside of his family, and Sorina wondered if Amers would be taken in. And if so, what he would do.

Her eyes moved involuntarily toward the room across the hall, where she knew Merrill and Jim Barlow were listening, via the slightly reworked intercom system, to everything that happened in the office. Even though she knew they were there, ready to come charging in in an instant if it became necessary, she was still nervous. It was not, however, the nervousness of physical fear. The nervousness came from the role she herself was to play, and she wondered if she could pull it off.

Other doubts, too, flitted through her mind—doubts about Amers' guilt, doubts about Merrill's and Barlow's activities—but she suppressed them easily. If Amers was, indeed, innocent of all charges, she was sure she would find out. She had realized, in fact, that that had been one of the reasons she had wanted to stay. She was, as the phony will required, an outside, impartial observer. Unlike Kathy Barlow, who was apparently totally convinced of his guilt, she would not try to railroad Amers.

When the doorbell sounded, she noticed that it was slightly less than ten minutes since the call to Amers. Taking a deep breath, she tossed the letter onto the desk, stood up, and went to the door.

Amers, as he stepped into the house, was still disheveled. His black hair was uncombed, and a dark shadow of beard covered the lower half of his face. His shirt was not fully tucked into his trousers.

He stopped just inside the door. "This had better be good," he said.

"Don't worry; it is," she replied as she turned to lead the way back to the office. "It's in the office."

"What's in the office?" He followed a few feet behind her.

"You'll see. It's better I show you than tell you."

He started to say something, but closed his mouth after an instant and remained silent as they walked down the hall and into the office. Sorina picked up the letter and handed it to him.

"Next to last paragraph," she said.

Amers glanced at her, frowning, then looked down at the paper.

"A letter?" he asked.

"A letter," she confirmed. "It doesn't look as if it was ever finished, certainly never mailed. If it had been, I imagine you would have heard about it before now."

His frown deepened, and he began to skim through the letter, slowing to read more carefully as he reached the paragraph she had pointed out to him. Some of the creases in his forehead smoothed out as he read silently, and then, as he neared the end, they returned, accompanied by a faint redness and a tightening of the muscles in his jaw.

He held it for a second after he was finished, then threw it on the desk.

"What the *hell* is that supposed to be?"

"What does it look like to you?"

His frown became a scowl, and one of the ridges of muscle in his jaw twitched.

"It looks," he said slowly and deliberately, "as if the Howalds are trying to get me, even after they're dead. That's what it looks like. Where did you get it?"

She gestured at the desk. "In one of the drawers. It looks as if Abel—if he's the one who wrote it—was sidetracked and never got back to finishing it. Or mailing it."

"It's no wonder he never mailed it, a damned lie like that!"

"But why should he have written it at all if it's all a lie?"

Amers shook his head angrily. "How the hell should I know?" His voice was tight with suppressed violence, the desire to lash out at something or someone who was now beyond his reach. His fingers were continuously clenching and unclenching, and Sorina wondered: From anger alone? Or from guilt as well?

"There's no truth to it at all?" Sorina asked quietly, looking up at him from where she still sat on the arm of the easy chair in the corner of the room.

He spun to face her. "Is that all you dragged me out of bed for? This piece of—of—"

He snatched up the letter again, held it in a trembling hand for a moment, involuntarily crumpling it. "Is that all?"

"You didn't answer me," Sorina persisted, still in a soft, reserved voice. "Is there any truth in it? Any truth at all?"

He stared down at her, his whole body rigid, his eyes smoldering. Convulsively, he threw the paper on the floor.

Suddenly, without warning, he laughed, harshly, explosively, and Sorina jerked backward a fraction of an inch.

"And if it *was* the truth, what kind of fool do you think I am that I would admit it? Do I look like a total idiot?" He spread his arms in an angry shrug. "So what good will it do me to deny anything? Will you believe me? Will *you*, who are being paid by Howald money, believe an Amers?"

"I'm not being paid *that* much by them, I assure you."

Amers snorted and turned back to the desk, stared at it a second, and spun back to face her again. "So you say, but how am I to know that *you're* telling the truth?"

"You could talk to Jerry Hunter, or Barbara Strickland, either one. They're the ones who are paying me—or will be in a few days, when I get my first check."

"Sure, they could tell me what you will be getting—

through them! But who's to say how much you're getting from the Howalds on the side? Or that you weren't working for them even before you came here?"

"All right," she said, shrugging. "we can't convince each other of anything. Is that about the way it stands?"

"That is exactly the way it stands!"

She was silent for several seconds, then asked, "You won't object, then, if I pass this on to Merrill Howald?"

"Of course I would object! Who wouldn't object to vicious lies about himself being made public?" He shrugged. "But what can I do to stop you?"

Now, she thought, now is the time to hit him with the proposal, the blackmail. Instead, she said, "Convince me that they're lies. Give me a reason for Abel to have written this if he hadn't actually suspected you."

He studied her closely, and some of the rigidness and tension seemed to drain out of him.

"You're serious?" he asked. "You really want me to give you a reason? Why?"

"Why not? Doesn't it sound fair to you?"

"Fair? Since when has a Howald been fair?"

"But I'm not a Howald. You keep forgetting that."

He studied her in silence for several seconds. "No, I suppose you're not," he said finally. "At least you don't *appear* to be."

"All right, then. How about a reason, then? And don't tell me it's just that the Howalds have had it in for the Amers for three generations. That sounds, if you'll pardon my saying so, just a bit paranoid."

Though she remained outwardly calm, her last comment had made her twitch slightly on the inside, as she half expected it to bring forth another explosion from Amers.

But it didn't. Amers stood over her, and for a moment all the tenseness seemed to return, but by the time he spoke, only seconds later, he seemed perfectly calm, his voice easy and level.

"All right," he said, "let's say, just for the sake of argument, that you really do want to give me an even break." He lowered himself onto one corner of the desk, glancing down at the partially crumpled piece of paper on the floor.

"Let's even say that Abel Howald really *did* suspect me of something," he went on. "But as you pointed out, he never mailed the letter with the accusations. It's possible, I suppose, that there really was some money diverted from one of his companies. If so, I can only wish the diverter well, whoever he or she is. But it wasn't me. As for why Abel suspected me—why not? Just as I am the third generation of Amerses to consider the Howalds as persecutors, Abel was the third generation of Howalds to consider the Amerses as thieves, regardless of what the facts are. What would be more natural? 'Somebody stole something from me; it must have been one of that thieving Amers clan!' You will notice," he went on, gesturing at the crumpled paper, "that even Abel commented on 'history repeating itself.' "

Amers shrugged. "The history was false the first time; it was false this time. And, as I said, you will note that the letter was not mailed. It could be that Abel found out who the real thief was, don't you think? Then, naturally, he wouldn't have mailed the letter."

"Possible," Sorina admitted. But the letter *had* been mailed, she thought to herself. "But why wouldn't he have destroyed the letter, then?"

"Who knows? I'm afraid I can't put myself in his place. Perhaps he just didn't think of it. After all, it wasn't anything important. Just something that could ruin a man's reputation if it got out."

Sorina was silent for a time, considering the advisability of her next words.

"I don't want to sound skeptical," she said, "but that still sounds a little weak, even a little paranoid."

Instead of exploding, Amers only smiled abruptly. "You know, Sorina, this would be funny if it weren't so serious. It really would. Look, if you're convinced you should give that paper to Howald or to the sheriff, or whoever you want—go right ahead. I'll survive."

"I'm glad you feel that way about it," she said quietly. "I don't think there's much I can do about it anyway, not legally. After all, the letter, along with all the other papers, will very probably belong to Merrill Howald as soon as the will is settled."

Unexpectedly, Amers laughed again, and Sorina glanced up, startled. "You found something amusing after all?" she asked.

"In a manner of speaking. You said they will probably belong to Merrill Howald soon. Well, let me give you another theory about that letter and why it was written but never mailed. And if you think I sounded paranoid before, just wait till you hear this one."

"Yes?" She watched him carefully as he leaned down and picked up the paper and carefully straightened it.

"Very simple," Amers said, spreading his hands before him as if he were presenting something physical to her. "Abel didn't write it."

"If he didn't write it, who did?" She couldn't completely suppress a start.

"Merrill Howald, who else?"

An odd feeling, half surprise, half disbelief, poured over her. "Merrill Howald? But why? And how?"

"How is simple enough. He was in town for days before you arrived. What was to stop him from writing it and planting it in the desk where you would be sure to find it?"

"Nothing. But why? Just to 'get you'?"

"If so, I'm paranoid, right? Well, let's say he had another reason. Let's say, for instance, that he's just adding a little cover-up for insurance."

"Covering up what?" she asked when he had been silent a few seconds. "What could he be covering up?"

"How about murder? Would that be good enough?"

"Murder? What murder?"

"His brother's murder, of course. What else?"

This time Sorina was unable to keep the surprise from her face and voice. "You're saying Merrill Howald killed his brother? And the others?"

He shrugged. "I'm just giving you reasons why that letter might have been written, that's all. Anyway, what's impossible about it? I remember a few days ago you were expressing doubts about the escaped convict theory yourself."

"Yes, but—"

"But nothing!" He stopped, grinning. "You know, the more I think about this, the better I like it. I think I may owe you something for dragging me over here in the middle of the night. I really do."

The grin spread as he went on, beginning to pace the floor as he talked.

"How does this grab you? Merrill Howald *hired* William Barlow to escape and kill Abel and his family? Believe me, he could afford it. And once he collects the whole estate . . . *That's* why Barlow came here when he had no logical reason to. And that's why he was able to disappear so thoroughly—he had *lots* of money, and maybe some help waiting for him."

"But why should Merrill—"

Amers laughed. "For the estate, of course! Don't forget, he was the younger brother, and he got damned little compared to Abel. But plenty, mind you, to use as a down payment to Barlow! And now this, just a little insurance. Just in case—now that he's showing himself and actually collecting the estate—just in case enough people start questioning the escaped convict idea—which they have been doing from the day it first came up—here we have a handy little clue pointing away from Merrill Howald. Toward me! 'That crook Amers, just like his grandfather. Got his hand caught in the till, and then slaughtered a whole family to cover it up!' "

He stopped pacing, staring down at her, still grinning. "Go ahead, tell Merrill about it. He'll be expecting you to! If you don't, he'll soon start wondering why. He may even have to stop by one of these days and 'discover' it himself."

Another laugh, and he went on. "But I wouldn't tell him about my theory, if I were you. I have the distinct suspicion that it wouldn't be safe. Of course, my offer of the loan of a gun still stands . . ."

She shook her head. "No, I don't think so. I . . ."

She glanced toward the door, toward the room across the hall where Merrill Howald and James Barlow waited, listening. She couldn't help but wonder what they thought now. Tables had been almost completely turned on them.

"All right," Amers said. "Well, if you don't have any more news for me tonight, I'll be getting back home. Once again, thanks for calling me. And if you come across any more papers like that, be sure to let me know."

He stepped out into the hall. "Just be careful what you tell—or don't tell—Merrill. Don't let him know you suspect anything—if, of course, you actually believe any of my wild speculations. Maybe you still think I'm not only a paranoid and an embezzler but a murderer as well." He shrugged and turned to go. "Just be careful, and don't say I didn't warn you. And the gun offer is still open."

He stopped, turned back for a second. "Who knows, if you have the gun around, you might not only survive—you might even save the state the cost of a trial. With any luck at all."

With a final laugh, Amers was gone, and a minute later she heard the front door slam.

The door across the hall opened, and Merrill looked down the hall cautiously. After a few seconds he stepped out and crossed the hall to the office. A few feet behind him came James Barlow.

Or . . .

The thought struck her abruptly. *Was* it James Barlow? Or was it, as she had thought when she had first glimpsed him, *William* Barlow? She had only his and

Merrill's word for who he was. She had only their word for everything.

James Barlow? Or William Barlow, returned to help Merrill wrap up the loose ends?

With an effort she stood up to meet the two men as they entered the room.

10

"You heard, I assume." Sorina forced a lightness into her voice that she didn't feel.

Merrill nodded as Barlow entered the room after him. Barlow was silent, his eyes not meeting Sorina's.

"I heard," he said, "and I can't say it was totally unexpected. I didn't expect him to be able to twist it so completely and so rapidly, though."

Merrill stopped, frowning slightly. "But I must say, you didn't push him very hard. What happened to that scheming little blackmailer we spent the last couple of days designing?"

"I'm sorry," Sorina apologized, "but I told you I'd have to play it by ear. Maybe I can do better tomorrow, or the day after. Whenever we 'find' some more evidence."

"I suppose you're right. The way he came up with those explanations, we'll really need something spectacular before you can threaten him effectively. And even then . . ." He shook his head. "I begin to suspect we underestimated him. Unless we can really shake him, he's not going to do anything but laugh at us."

"What's next for me?" Sorina asked. "What paper do I find next?"

Merrill shook his head. "I don't know. I thought I had it all planned out, but that was before he reacted the way he did. It's going to be harder than I thought. But don't worry, we'll come up with something in a day or two."

Just like Norris Amers said you would, she couldn't help but think, but she said nothing.

The next day she drove to the post office in Elston

and took a close look at the poster still displayed for William Barlow. The results were inconclusive. The picture was several years old, for one thing. For another, the hair was different. At the time the poster picture had been taken, William Barlow's hair had been short, practically a crew cut, parted peremptorily on one side. James Barlow's hair, on the other hand, was considerably longer and not parted at all. James Barlow *might* be William Barlow, grown older, with longer hair and a slightly receding hairline, or he might be someone who looked a lot like William Barlow—someone like a brother.

After the post office, Sorina drove to the prison farm again. According to their records, Ormand said, William Barlow did have a brother named James, who had, at the time of Barlow's imprisonment, lived five hundred miles away. There was also mention of a sister, but as far as Ormand knew, neither had ever visited Barlow, though they had corresponded regularly. Barlow had kept none of the letters, though. At least, none had been found in his belongings, although Ormand conceded that Barlow could have taken them with him in anticipation of his escape. Ormand had never seen the letters, so he had no idea what the correspondence had been about.

Just before noon Sorina returned to Elston and talked briefly with the sheriff. He had little to add to what she already knew. He was aware of the various theories, but declined to say he put much faith in any of them.

"If a guy killed once, no matter what the circumstances, chances are he's capable of killing again. The second one is always easier. If you want my opinion, Barlow went out to the Howald place looking for money. Something happened to set him off, and he killed them all and ran, too scared to look around for the money after that. Or maybe, the way he disappeared, he got his hands on a big chunk of cash they had laying around the house that nobody knew about.

You never know, someone with that much money might leave a thousand bucks laying around like you or me'd leave fifty cents on the dresser."

He shook his head as he rose to usher Sorina out of his office. "Take my word for it, Miss Stark, ninety-nine times out of a hundred, it's the simplest explanation that's true. Most killings are spur-of-the-moment things, and there's no complicated plans involved. Somebody gets the wrong button pushed in his head, and he goes off, that's all."

Mrs. Strickland wasn't much more help. She remembered Barlow vaguely from when the whole family had lived at the south end of Elston. She *thought* she remembered him having some brothers and sisters, but it was all a long time ago. Everyone but William had moved away a year or so before Barlow had gotten in the brawl that had ended in the death of Jay Horton, who had the reputation, when drunk, of being the town bully. Barlow had apparently lucked out and landed a lucky punch, but the luck had gone a little too far when Horton's head smashed against something.

As for Merrill Howald, Mrs. Strickland didn't have much to say either. He had been back in Elston very little since he had gone away to college, but from what she remembered of him, he had always "seemed like a nice boy." Neither did she have anything bad to say about Norris Amers, and she was strictly neutral on the origins of the feud between the families. She had heard both sides of the story, and, so she said, gave no more weight to one than the other. "After all, anyone involved with history should be impartial."

In the end, of course, it was Sorina's decision and hers alone, and for once in her life she couldn't make up her mind. She would, she decided, simply have to continue to play it by ear and see what developed.

Back at the house, she talked for a few minutes with Barlow, who was now "standing guard" almost continuously, just to be on the safe side, though no one seriously thought that Amers was shaken enough to do anything foolish. In fact, the way things stood after last night's reversal, Merrill seemed perhaps more shaken than Amers, and Barlow, though he remained stoic and calm on the surface, gave Sorina the feeling that it would take little to make him explode.

Since the paper-sorting part of the job had now been revealed as a phony, it was pointless for her to continue with that effort. So, in early afternoon, Sorina decided to take a walk around the neighborhood and talk to a few of the nearby neighbors to see if any of them knew anything at all about the cat, which, strangely enough, had not put in an appearance on either of the nights since it had led her out to the orchard in the middle of the night. The day was crisp and clear with only a slight breeze, so, if nothing else, she would get a couple of hours of pleasant exercise walking from place to place.

The closest she came to finding out anything worthwhile was at the Hennings' place, a half mile down the road to the west, which was where Barlow's prison clothes had been found. Joetta Henning, a slender girl of about twelve, was in the back yard practicing flips and splits for the cheerleader tryouts the next day. She had, she said as she did a handstand without breaking her train of thought, seen a cat like that off and on all spring and summer, ever since the weather had been good enough for her to get out. It seemed to stick pretty close to the old Howald place, though, she said. At least that was the only place she'd ever seen it.

She came back down on her feet and looked up at Sorina a little nervously, as if not quite sure she should have admitted trespassing. "I sort of wondered who it belonged to," she said. "It had that really pretty collar—I never saw one like that before. Does it still have it?"

Sorina nodded, and a thought crossed her mind. "Did you ever take food down to it?"

The girl lowered her eyes. "Once or twice," she said, "but it never ate any of it, so I quit. I s'pose it must catch a lot of mice and things. It's out around the barn and the orchard a lot."

"You never saw it anywhere else? Not along the road? Or at anyone else's house?"

She shook her head. "No place else. I tried to bring it home with me once, but it wouldn't come. It just started crying whenever I tried to take it anywhere. I thought maybe it had some kittens somewhere, but I never could find any." She looked up at Sorina hopefully. "You see any?"

"No, I've just seen the cat itself. The funny thing, though, is that it seems to get in and out of the house whenever it wants to. You didn't ever see it coming from some particular place around the house, did you?"

"No, the only place I ever saw it was out around the orchard, and the barns, like I said. But mostly the orchard."

Mostly the orchard. The same place the cat had tried to lead Sorina at least twice. (Hadn't it?)

Mostly the orchard . . .

Sorina was walking across the bridge at the east end of the drive when Norris Amers pulled up in his car. He stopped before the bridge and got out.

"Hi," he said, half waving, half saluting as he moved toward her. "Any more discoveries amongst the archives that I should know about?" His words were jaunty, his voice exuberant.

She shook her head. "Nothing today. To tell the truth, I haven't been looking much."

"Oh? Your mind on other, higher things today?"

"Not really. For one thing, I've been thinking about what you said last night."

"And the logic of it overwhelmed you, no doubt."

"Not completely, but I have to admit there's a certain sense to what you say. I was talking to the sheriff, though, and he seems completely satisfied that everything was as it appeared to be—Barlow went off the deep end, killed them, and got away."

Amers shrugged. "Why not? Anything is possible. Our sheriff, though, has never been noted for his imagination. In any event, his version and mine don't differ by that much. The only difference is, I suggested that Barlow was paid to go off the deep end. That's all. And now that I've had a day to think the idea over, it sounds even better than it did last night. In fact, if you and Howald don't take that letter to the sheriff, I think I'll tell him about it myself."

"You really want me to tell Merrill about it?" She eyed him suspiciously.

"Why not? Even if I were to give him the benefit of the doubt and say that he *didn't* plant that so-called letter, what could he do with it? It isn't signed, for one thing. For another, it presents only unfounded suspicions. Not a fact in the whole thing. So what harm is there in it? None to me, certainly."

"All right," she said abruptly, "I will. This evening. We'll see what happens *then*."

Amers grinned. "Very good. It should prove interesting. Incidentally, my offer of the gun still goes. You're sure you won't take me up on it? I'd hate to see anything happen to a pretty thing like you."

"No, thanks," she said, "I'll see if I can get along without one."

He shrugged. "It's your decision. Just remember the offer is always open. Just give me a call whenever you feel the need."

"I'll keep it in mind," she said, "but now—"

She broke off as the cat appeared, the gem in its collar glittering in the afternoon sun. It was a dozen yards away, not far from the corner of East House. Amers glanced in the direction in which she was looking.

"It's back, eh?" he said. "I don't suppose you found out who it belongs to?"

"No, but according to Joetta Henning, just down the road, it's been here for several months, at least since spring." She watched the cat for a minute as it sat in the grass, staring toward them. Sorina couldn't be sure at this distance, but its eyes seemed to be centering on Amers, not herself. Then, as they watched, it slowly got up and walked away, looking back toward them as it moved.

"Come on," she said suddenly to Amers, "I swear that cat is trying to lead me somewhere. I'm going to find out once and for all. You want to come along?"

He looked at her oddly, then shrugged. "Why not? Incidentally, did you ever find out how it was getting in and out of the house?"

"No," she said as they moved off the drive and into the grass, "I checked everything twice, but not a clue. And Merrill says there aren't any secret panels. None that he knows of, at least."

Amers laughed. "You want me to take a look? Maybe I could do a little better than Mr. Howald."

She didn't answer. Several yards ahead of them the cat had moved around the corner of East House, and by the time they reached that corner, the cat was rounding the next one, and then was moving on through the shrubs and trees that crowded around the gazebo. As Sorina had expected, the cat was heading once again for the narrow bridge to the orchard.

"Where's it going?" Amers wanted to know. "Do you have any idea?"

"The orchard, unless things have changed," she said.

"Orchard? What could there be back there?" A frown forced several creases into his forehead, and abruptly the exuberance was gone from his voice.

"I don't know, but that's where it always goes. And Joetta said the only places she ever saw it in the last few months were the orchard and the barns."

Amers hung back as they approached the maze of shrugs and trees around the gazebo. He laughed.

"Are you serious about this?" There was a touch of incredulity in his voice. "You don't really think a cat would lead you to anything, do you?"

Sorina shrugged as she continued moving ahead. "I've given up being logical with this animal, the way it seems to get through solid walls to get in and out of the house. Right now I'm just curious. If you don't want to come, you don't have to."

"I didn't say that," he said hastily, and fell in behind her again, hurrying to catch up. "I just can't imagine what you expect to find."

"Who knows? A treasure trove of dead mice or squirrels. Maybe some kittens. Joetta said she thought it might have had kittens last spring."

But was that all? Was that really the only reason? Or was there something else that drew her now? Something that she hadn't yet admitted to her rational mind . . .

Ahead, the cat had reached the small bridge leading across the stream to the orchard. It paused at the far end before plunging ahead into the tall grass.

"The same as before," Sorina commented as they reached the bridge themselves and crossed over. "The time before, it headed over that way—" She laughed. "The same way it's heading now."

As they watched, it moved between the trees, at times visible only as a swaying of the tall grass around it, at others as a flash of white as it leaped over a hidden obstacle.

Then it stopped. From where they stood near the bridge, they could hear a faint mewing.

"Looks like that's the destination," Sorina commented, and began pushing her way through the grass. She looked back at Amers, who still stood at the bridge, silently.

"It doesn't look like this has been mowed at all this year, not like the rest of the grounds," she said.

His eyes drifted toward her. "No," he said absently, "no one ever comes out here, and we thought it might look better if it grew wild. Like a small forest."

She nodded. "Nice idea. Are you coming to look at the treasure?"

He shook his head. "No, you go ahead; I—"

Again there was the mewing sound, now only a few feet from where Sorina walked. She could see the cat, sitting in an open space among the trees. The grass and weeds seemed slightly less thick for an area of a few square feet. As she approached, the cat mewed again, then stuck its nose to the ground for a moment. A second later its tail arched high and it began to dig.

Sorina came and stood next to the animal, and she could see a small pile of dirt near its back feet. It stopped digging and looked up. For an instant Sorina had the odd feeling that somehow it was going to speak to her, so expressive seemed the eyes.

But the feeling passed, and as she knelt down, the cat backed away and sat watching her.

"This is it, cat? This is what all the fuss was about?" She shook her head. "You're a disappointment, cat. You'll never make Lassie-grade this way."

She stood up and turned back toward the house, only to almost collide with Amers, who apparently had decided to take a closer look at the cat's destination after all. His face seemed drawn and tight, and it was hard to believe the change that had come over it in the last few minutes.

"Is something wrong?" Sorina asked.

He shook his head. "No, nothing." He glanced around, his eyes locating the cat, still sitting a couple of yards away. But now, Sorina noticed, its ears were drawn back almost flat against its head, and it was crouching low in the grass.

"You two just don't get along, that's all there is to it," Sorina said lightly, "but don't take it to heart. I can't get along with dogs myself."

A nervous smile flickered on his lips and was gone. "What was it?" he asked. "What did it have back here?"

"Nothing," she said, "not a thing. It just stopped, right there—see that little bare spot?—and started digging."

"Digging?" He swallowed once, and then seemed to recover. "What would it be digging for?"

Sorina shrugged. "I don't know. A ground hog? A

mole? What do outdoors cats dig for? My experience has been mostly with indoor cats, and all they dig in is their litter pans. And the furniture."

"It could be an animal, I suppose," Amers said after a moment. "I can't imagine what else it could be."

He moved a step forward, toward the cat. There was a deep-throated growl, and the animal crouched even lower and seemed to slither backward an inch or two as if trying to burrow into the very ground.

Amers stood silently, staring down at the cat, then at the bare spot on the ground and the tiny pile of dirt. He swallowed once, then shrugged and turned away.

"Cats are strange animals," he said, a little stiffly. "I've never cared much for them. Maybe this one can sense it."

"Possible," Sorina admitted. "I've heard that cats are sensitive in some ways, but this seems a little extreme. Are you sure you've never seen it before?"

He shook his head, perhaps a bit more vehemently than necessary. "Not before the other night," he said, "in the house."

He began walking back toward the bridge. Behind him, the cat seemed to relax slightly, its ears once again cocked, the faint growl dying away. Its eyes shifted to Sorina, and once again there was the uncanny feeling that the animal was about to speak to her.

She shook her head briskly and turned to follow Amers, who by now had reached the bridge. He crossed it without looking back, and Sorina followed him more slowly. Behind her she could hear the faint mewing of the cat. . . .

Sorina opened her eyes to darkness. For a moment the dream images held and danced before her eyes like a fading memory. And then, despite an almost physical effort to grasp them, they were gone, and she was alone in the blackness.

But no, she was not. She felt the weight on her legs,

the shifting weight of a small body that moved restlessly back and forth.

She started to laugh in the darkness as she realized that, once again, the cat had found its way to her bedroom, but the laughter froze in her throat as she remembered:

On this night she had closed and locked the bedroom door.

And somewhere in the house, she knew, was James (or was it William?) Barlow, standing guard.

She snapped on the bedside light, and instantly came the thump as the cat bounded to the floor. It raced to the door—which was still closed. And the key, she saw, was still on the bedside table, next to the lamp.

For a long moment she sat propped up on her elbows in bed, her heart beginning to pound. The door *had* to be open!

Unless it had been opened and closed before she had awakened.

But how? And by whom?

Then, as she sat there, her mind whirling, the smell reached her nostrils. It was faint at first, unrecognizable, but rapidly it grew stronger, more distinctive.

Smoke!

Instantly she leaped from the bed, pausing only long enough to stuff her feet into the slippers. She grasped the door knob, twisted, but nothing happened. The cat stood by, only inches from her feet, looking up anxiously.

She grabbed the key from the bedside table, and pushed it into the lock, and twisted.

Nothing happened. It wouldn't turn! The lock must be jammed somehow, she thought. But how could that be? It had worked only hours before, quickly and easily.

She tried again, twisting at the key until the edges bit into her finger, but still it would not turn.

The phone, she thought suddenly. At least she could call the fire department, and they would be here in a few minutes. After all, Elston was less than five miles away. That, certainly, would be soon enough to get her out.

She snatched up the receiver and thrust her finger into the dial, waiting tensely for the dial tone. A second went by, then two, then ten, and there was only silence.

There was no dial tone.

In her nostrils the smell of smoke was growing stronger.

11

What the *hell*, she wondered, was going on? The lock jammed? The phone out of order? And a fire somewhere in the house?

Forcing herself to be calm, she tapped at the prongs sticking up from the phone's cradle. Perhaps, just perhaps, they might be stuck.

But they were not. They operated perfectly. The phone was simply dead.

At her feet that cat moved back and forth rapidly, restlessly, mewing as it paced.

"All right," she said, thinking aloud, "keep calm. It's going to work out." She looked down at the animal. "I don't know how you got in here, cat, but I'm damned glad you did. At least I'm awake . . ."

She hung up the useless phone, took a deep breath, and looked around. The smell of smoke was stronger and—was it her imagination?—she thought she could hear the crackling of the flames.

The window, she thought. It couldn't be more than fifteen feet above the ground . . .

Moving quickly but forcing herself not to run, she went to the window and looked out. The nearest tree was a dozen feet away.

She tried to raise the window, but it wouldn't move. A quick look at the top and sides showed her why. It had been painted shut long ago. And why not? With air conditioning, who ever opened windows?

She hurried back to the door, felt it briefly. It wasn't hot, which meant the fire was not in the hall outside yet—not burning freely, at least. She glanced down at herself, at the pajamas and loose, floppy slippers. If she was going to climb out the window, after she broke it, she would never make it to the ground wearing these slippers. She had a *little* time left, thanks to the cat's waking her up, so . . .

Once dressed, in heavy slacks and sweater and a pair of tennis shoes, she grabbed up her battered suitcase and took it to the window. Pushing the cat away with her foot and shielding her face with one arm, she swung the suitcase into the window.

Glass shattered, most of it falling outside, but some bouncing back into the room. Fresh air flooded in, carrying away the odor of smoke, but outside, on the trees, she could see the flickering redness of the light from the flames. With the edge of the suitcase, she knocked out all the jagged glass from the edges of the window, and then turned back to the bed.

Insane, she told herself as she yanked the bedspread off, then the blanket and both sheets. She had never been much good at knot tying, but she managed, and she soon had something that would get her so close to the ground that she wouldn't break a leg when she let go.

Next she slid the bed closer to the window, wondering where the strength was coming from, and then tied the free end of the bedspread to the leg next to the window. With it fastened, she threw the improvised rope out the window.

And the cat—

Startled, Sorina looked around. It was nowhere to be seen.

"Come on, cat! You probably saved my life; I'm not leaving you up here."

The closet? No, that was empty.

For an instant she dropped down on all fours and looked under everything—bureau, bed, chairs, bedside table. But there was nothing, no cat.

"All right, cat, you're magic. Or did you—"

She leaned out the window. Below her and to the left, from the windows in the other half of the house, the flickering light from the flames was growing stronger.

And the cat! Sorina felt the hair at the back of her neck struggling to rise as she saw it, a few yards from the house, at the edge of the drive. Its eyes—and the carnelian in its collar—gleamed red in the flickering light.

Impossible! But its appearance in the room had been impossible, too, and yet it had been there.

And it had saved her life.

But there was no time to wonder how the cat did what it did—not now. The flames were growing steadily brighter, and she thought she could hear a crackling sound from somewhere beyond the door to her room.

Taking time only to throw her purse to the ground, she climbed into the window and, gripping the frame tightly, praying that she had cleared away all the tiny bits of glass, turned herself around until she was facing into the room, literally crouching on the windowsill.

Then, with one hand clamped painfully onto the frame, she took the sheet-rope in the other. Quickly, before she could lose her nerve, she shifted the other hand to the rolled-up sheet. For several seconds she squatted there, swaying slightly, her arms stretched rigidly in front of her, her knees almost touching her chin. Every muscle in her body, every nerve, seemed stretched to the breaking point.

Slowly she raised herself a few inches, then leaned back another few degrees, shifting her hands on the sheet in spasmodic jerks. Keeping one foot firmly on the windowsill, she lifted the other free and lowered it a few inches. She didn't look down, but probed for the wall with her foot.

At first she felt nothing; her foot touched only air, and she froze, her other leg trembling, her stomach heaving. She took a deep breath and swung her foot in farther—and touched the wall!

She sighed in relief as she pressed against the wall with her foot. But would it hold? Or would it slip when she moved the other leg, letting her crash against the bottom of the window frame as she fell?

Another deep breath. "Farther back," she told herself, "farther back."

Slowly she shifted her grip on the sheet again, letting more of it slide painfully through her fingers as she leaned frighteningly farther back, feeling the pressure on the critical foot mount as the strain on her arms increased.

"All right," she muttered half aloud, "that's enough. Get moving before your goddamn lousy knots give way!"

Tensing herself even more, she moved the second foot and brought it down to join the first against the wall. Nothing slipped, but the thought of trying it in her floppy slippers—or bare feet—shot through her mind, and she said a quick thanks for the ratty old tennis shoes that she had almost—but not quite!—thrown out before coming here to Elston.

From there on it was relatively easy, walking backward down the wall, easing herself along a few inches at a time.

Then she was dropping the last few feet, and as her toes hit the ground, every muscle in her body seemed to go limp, and she collapsed onto the grass.

She pulled in a half dozen deep breaths, closed her eyes for a moment. She was out! She was out!

Abruptly she sat up. The fire department! She still had to get the fire department! The flames were becoming brighter by the minute, and soon—

Her purse. She had to find her purse to get the keys so she could drive to a phone. She scrambled to her feet and looked around hastily.

There it was, at the edge of the drive. She grabbed it up and ran down the drive toward the garage—and stopped abruptly.

A car loomed up before her, parked almost directly in front of the main door to the house. But who—

Merrill! It was Merrill's car!

But what was he doing here? He hadn't even come to the house that evening. Instead, he had called to say that, what with Amers' suspicions, he had better stay away for a while, but that he was making good progress on the "hard evidence" they would need.

Not knowing why, she ran up the steps to the front door and peered through the narrow window at one side, squinting against the glare of the flames that filled much of the right half of the house and were now spreading rapidly up the stairs.

She looked—and gasped!

She felt as if someone had jabbed a grasping fist inside her body. Her stomach felt as if it were being twisted and pulled. Inside the building, stretched out at the left of the stairs, lay Merrill Howald, and next to him, a few feet away, was a gasoline can.

A few feet beyond, Sorina noticed almost as an afterthought, lay Barlow.

Both were obviously unconscious.

She grabbed and twisted at the knob. It turned, but the door would not budge, not without a key. She hadn't expected it to, not after the door in her room had been jammed.

The fire department, she thought sharply, but stopped.

It would be too late—too late by several minutes. For Merrill it was now or never. *She* would have to get him out!

But how? She could break the window in the back door, or one of the other windows, but would that do any good? She could get inside, but what then? The doors both operated the same way, needing a key to get both in and out, and if, as in her own room, the keys didn't work . . .

Frantically she tore open her purse and dug through it—and remembered!

The keys to the house were in her room on the second floor, on the bureau top. She had tossed them there, where they had lain hidden by her purse as she grabbed it and threw it through the open window.

But at least her car keys . . .

Running through the flickering, flaming night, she reached her car, parked just outside the garage doors. Thank heavens she had been too lazy to put it away when she had gotten back from that movie in Elston.

But it would be too late! Even as the engine coughed and stuttered into life, she knew that by the time she reached a phone and got the fire department here, it would be too late. The flames were spreading too rapidly! Both men would be finished long before a fire engine could get here!

But what could she do? Her mind raced uselessly and her stomach churned. Merrill was too heavy for her to heave over any of the windowsills, she was positive.

No, there was no way. The best she could hope to do was drag them, and that wouldn't—

She slammed on the brakes, and the car skidded to a stop in the curve of the gravel drive.

The back door! Unlike the front door, which had a half dozen steps leading up to it, the back door was on ground level. If she could get the car around there, and—

Well, she thought as she jammed the car into reverse and the wheels spit gravel against the underside, it's contract time. She had told herself often enough in the last few days that she should be cautious when it came to making any kind of "contract" with Merrill Howald, but now there was no more time to be cautious. If she didn't do something fast, Merrill would be dead. There would be no one for her to "contract" with.

The headlights swept across the lawn and then onto the west corner of the house. The lawn, though slightly hilly, looked smooth enough. She moved forward, steering around the trees at what seemed a breakneck pace. She squeezed the car between another pair of trees with only a foot to spare, and then another, and finally she was at the back of the house. Here the going was tighter, but still she swerved on, and in less than a minute her lights shone on the back door.

Okay, she thought, this is it. We'll see how good you are, you old wreck!

She backed, maneuvered, straining at the steering wheel with a strength she didn't know she had, until the car was lined up so that—she hoped!—the right front fender and bumper would smash into the door at about a forty-five-degree angle. For a second she sat there, but just a second. No time for wondering. It would work or it wouldn't. And if it didn't work the first time . . .

She pushed the accelerator down sharply, all the way to the floor.

There were only a few feet to go when she started, but they turned out to be more than enough. The right headlight was shattered, the fender crumpled, and she heard the grating sound she had come to dread when she was learning to park.

But the door toppled inward a moment later, as the car came to a shuddering rest nosed up against the door frame. Hastily she shifted into reverse, hoping it still worked.

It did, despite the crumpled look, and she stopped after a few feet. She leaped out and dashed for the door.

The fire covered most of the stairs, licking the air only inches from Merrill. As she went forward, an arm raised in front of her face to ward off the heat, an icy calm gripped her, as if she were watching another, unrelated person move toward the flames.

Without checking to see if there were any signs of life, she grabbed Merrill by the shoulders, but discovered immediately that his upper body was too heavy for her to lift easily, leaving her bent over so far that she couldn't even drag him.

She dropped his shoulders and grabbed his feet. That worked better, but it was still hard going. She cursed the heavy nap on the rug, wishing desperately that it was bare wood.

But she made it. Somehow she made it, dragging him past the shattered door, across the narrow, concrete patio, and onto the cold, damp grass in the glare of the single headlight.

And she went back. Barlow was closer to the door, but by now the fire had completely enveloped the stairs and was advancing rapidly down the other hall. The heat . . .

Keeping low, shielding her face, she managed to reach him, put one hand out to grasp at his limp, outstretched hand.

But she couldn't move him. His weight, and that damned, thick rug!

Then suddenly she was thrust aside, and a bass voice, trembling and shaking, rang out over the crackling of the flames.

"Get the hell out of here! I'll get him!"

"Merrill!"

The cold ground, the dragging, the night air—something—must have brought him around, and now he lurched past her, stooping low, his head down to keep the heat from his face and eyes. He grasped Barlow's hand, the one Sorina had just abandoned, and pulled. He dragged him slowly, straining to keep ahead of the flames as they licked out even farther from the stairs and appeared now out of the ceiling itself.

Sorina herself, more than glad to be relieved of having to make further attempts at moving Barlow's massive body, had turned and stumbled out through the door and now leaned heavily against the crumpled fender of her car, breathing hard and feeling surprised that she was still able to stand.

Once outside the door, away from the direct glare and heat of the flames, Merrill stopped and released Barlow's arms. For several seconds he stood silently, breathing in the outside air in huge gasps.

"Get that out of the way!" he said, gesturing at the car. "This whole wall could go any minute!"

For a moment she didn't move, didn't react. And then she remembered, "The fire department! I was going to—"

"Never mind! Let the damn thing burn! Just get out of the way. We have to get Jim—"

He stopped. In the distance there came the faint wail of sirens.

"Someone must have seen it," Merrill said. "They can take Jim to the hospital."

Then, with a final deep breath, he squatted down, forced both arms under Barlow's limp form, and straightened up. He staggered slightly as he moved across the patio and onto the ground, past the car.

As Merrill moved farther back, away from the building, away from the flames that were now erupting from the second-floor windows, Sorina got into the car unsteadily and backed it away from the house, through the trees.

Slowly, haltingly, as if his strength were almost gone, Merrill lowered Barlow to the ground near the car, a good hundred feet back from the house. The man was motionless where he lay.

Merrill slowly stood up, straightening himself stiffly, breathing heavily. He stood silently for a moment, his eyes playing over the burning building. He said something under his breath, and then at a slow jog started around toward the front of the flaming building. The sirens were much louder now, and, looking past the corner of the house, Sorina could see a flashing red light down the road, probably near the Henning house.

Who, she wondered, had turned in the alarm? Amers? Or someone at the Henning place? Or just someone driving by? But it didn't matter. The fire engines were turning into the front drive now, and that was all that mattered. West House would be a total loss, but at least the others could be saved.

And Merrill was apparently all right, and Barlow . . .

She knelt down next to the man, looking closely for the first time. It was difficult to see in the flickering light from the burning house and the glow of the single headlight, but she noticed two things almost at once. First, his chest was moving in a regular pattern, and second, a path of blood, now darkened and nearly dry, ran along one side of his face, starting from somewhere above his ear and running jaggedly forward onto his cheek.

And for the first time since she had awakened—how long ago had it been? Was it possible only a few minutes had passed?—some of the significance of what had happened began to push into her mind.

The fire itself, the locked doors, both men unconscious on the floor, the gasoline can. Arson? Attempted murder?

She looked up as she heard voices and the sound of feet pounding rapidly across the ground. From around the corner of the house came Merrill, followed closely by a fireman, bulky in his protective clothing. Sorina stood up and moved back from Barlow as the two approached.

Merrill came to stand next to Sorina as the fireman knelt hurriedly next to Barlow, hastily checking pulse and respiration and briefly lifting the eyelids.

"We better all get around to the front," he said, standing up. "An ambulance should be here in a few minutes."

Merrill moved forward, making as if to help move Barlow, but the fireman motioned him back. "I can handle him. You two just take it easy and come around to the front. You better get yourselves checked over, too."

The fireman, several inches shorter than Merrill but much broader, knelt down, slid his arms under Barlow's knees and shoulders, and stood up. Barlow's head flopped back limply, and the fireman shifted his grip to support it as he started toward the front of the house.

Merrill followed, taking Sorina's arm as he moved forward.

"Come on," he said, "he's right about being looked over."

She nodded and tried to match his steps, questions bubbling through her mind. Then abruptly, before she could ask any of them, she stopped. Merrill's hand on her arm nearly pulled her off her feet before he realized she had stopped.

"What happened?" He looked down at her, frowning worriedly.

For an answer, she only pointed. Sitting a few feet away, near the base of a tree, was the cat. Its eyes glinted red in the light from the flames, and the carnelian glowed like a bloody, third eye. As they looked at it, the cat began to yowl.

"That's the cat? So . . . ?" Merrill put pressure on her arm. "Come on, we'd better do as he said, and—"

Suddenly, violently, Sorina shook her head.

"What?" Merrill stared down at her, the frown deepening. "What's the matter?"

"That's what it was!" she said, half whispering. "It was the cat!"

"That's what *what* was? What the hell are you talking about?"

"Amers yesterday. He was so cocky, so sure of himself—until we followed the cat out to the orchard!"

"Orchard? What—"

"There's something out there! There has to be! Our phony papers didn't scare him, but whatever is out there in the orchard did! It scared the hell out of him! He must have thought—"

She stopped, looking up at him. "It *was* Amers who started the fire, wasn't it?"

"I don't know, but I suppose it must have been. I got a message saying I should come out here right away. I assumed it was from Jim, but it must have been Amers. I tried to call, but I couldn't get through, and when I got here, someone knocked me out."

He raised one hand and lightly, wincingly, touched a spot on the back of his head. "I don't know where the hell he was hiding, but he hit me almost as soon as I got out of the car. The next thing I remember is waking up out here and seeing you trying to drag Jim."

He was silent for a moment. "You know, it's just beginning to sink in. We almost ended up like Abel and his family . . . But you, what happened to you?"

"The cat woke me up and I smelled smoke. I couldn't get my door open, and the phone wouldn't work, so I managed to climb out the window. I saw you two inside, unconscious, and the only way I could think to get you out was what I did—knock down the door with my car."

"The cat woke you up? But if the door was locked, how—"

"I don't know. That's another reason I think there's something out there in the orchard. That cat has been trying to lead me out there since the first day I came here, and I've never been able to figure out how it gets in and out of the house. Getting into my room tonight was just one more impossibility on top of all the previous ones. And now . . ."

She looked toward the cat, which was still pacing beneath the tree, yowling with an almost Siamese-like intensity every few seconds. The sound was clearly audible over the crackle of the fire and the noises of the men and engines beyond the house.

"And now," she went on, "I'm going to find out just what's back there, whether you're coming or not."

"But—"

"I know all the arguments, believe me. They've been buzzing around in my head like a swarm of bees the last few seconds. But I'm going anyway, one way or another. Are you coming or not?"

He stared at her silently for several seconds, then sighed loudly.

"All right," he said, "but you'll need some light." He glanced toward the burning house. "You wait here. I'll see if I can maneuver my car around. I'd better get it out of the way of the firemen anyway."

"We'll need something to dig with, too," she said. "I'll meet you at the toolshed, down there." She waved a hand toward the small group of buildings behind the central house, just barely visible in the light from the flames that now seemed to be leaping out of every window in the house.

He looked as if he were going to object, but instead he turned and began walking rapidly toward the corner of the house. Sorina watched for a second and then turned in the opposite direction and made for the toolshed.

And as she did, the cat stopped its pacing and moved with her, paralleling her path a few feet farther from the house. Its face was turned toward her, the eyes—the *three* eyes—glinting and flickering, keeping time to the flames that leaped and flamed into the sky. And every few seconds it made the same eerie, deep-throated yowl . . .

The toolshed, when she reached it, was little more than a wavering shadow, and it was as much by feel as by sight that she located the sagging door that she remembered from the last time she had passed it. She pressed against the door, lightly at first, then more firmly, and she felt it give. It scraped back noisily across the rough wooden floor as she pushed.

Inside, her eyes adjusted and she could make out the familiar shapes of picks, rakes, hoes, a coiled garden hose, a shovel, and—from one corner she snatched up the spade and went back outside.

The cat was several feet away, toward the orchard, again pacing back and forth, its eyes fixed on Sorina's. And always, every few seconds, the yowl . . .

In the distance a pair of lights appeared and maneuvered their way toward her. As they approached, she hurried ahead of them, trotting through the grass, across one corner of the horse track, and to the creek at a point several yards past the bridge. She stopped and motioned the car forward, then went to the driver's side.

"There," she said, pointing to the spot to which she had been taken that afternoon, "it's right in there somewhere."

Merrill pulled the car forward almost to the edge of the creek and got out, leaving the lights on and the motor running. He started to say something, but stopped as he heard—and then saw—the cat, pacing several yards to one side of the car, near the bridge. He looked at Sorina for a moment, then reached out and took the spade from her hand.

They were silent as they walked, and for the first time Sorina wondered: A spirit? Clarice's spirit, leading them through the night, toward . . .

Toward what?

Involuntarily she shivered. From somewhere, as they crossed the narrow bridge, a cold wind seemed to blow, and ahead of them the cat turned to look back. It was as if, she thought, it was leading them into another world, a world bounded by the creek and the trees, turned by the headlights into an island isolated in the night. They could still hear the noises of the fire behind them, but it was remote, another dimension entirely, a world that could not affect them here.

For the second time in—what, twelve hours?—Sorina stood looking down at the spot where the cat had crouched, digging. There was silence now, except for the sounds of the fire that still drifted into their world.

"Here," she said, pointing toward the small bare spot of earth at her feet.

Merrill hesitated, glancing from Sorina to the cat, which now stood watching from the edge of the patch of light. After a moment he nodded and jabbed the shovel into the ground with a sound that was startlingly loud.

"All right! That's enough!"

Norris Amers stepped slowly into the island of light. The gun in his hand was pointed directly at Merrill.

12

"It *was* you, then," Merrill said, not moving, his hands still on the spade, which stood upright in the ground. "You did start the fire."

"What choice did you leave me?"

There was a strange quality to Amers' voice, slightly higher pitched than normal, with a tone that suggested that he was talking to a pair of children he had just caught with their hands in a cookie jar. Or was it the child itself that was speaking, with an adult voice, to an accusing adult audience that the child just could not bring itself to understand?

"What choice?'" Amers repeated more loudly. "I didn't want to do it, especially to you, Miss Stark—Sorina. It wasn't your fault that you became involved with *them!*" An edge of contempt cut through the last word.

"I suppose Abel left you no choice either," Merrill said quietly.

"None! 'Give it back!' he said, 'And we will forget about the whole ugly incident.' " Amers laughed harshly. "*Give it back!* As if he didn't owe me that much a thousand times over!"

"Our grandfathers," Merrill said, his deep voice soft and agreeable, but Sorina could see the tightness around his eyes. "Leroy and Aaron cheated your grandfather out of his share of the business, is that it?"

"You're damned right that's it!"

"But why the whole family? Why not just my brother?"

"She was with him in his judgment, so why shouldn't she remain with him in *my* judgment?"

"And the boy?" As Merrill spoke, Sorina realized for

the first time that he had moved. Each time he spoke, he eased himself forward and to one side, perhaps no more than an inch each time, but it was still a movement. Amers did not seem to notice.

"Another Howald!" Amers said, as if that were the answer to all questions.

Merrill was silent then, and Sorina plunged in. "What would we have found here," she asked, "if we had gone on digging?"

He turned his eyes on Sorina. For a moment she saw again what she had seen in his eyes that afternoon, and she realized now that it was fear.

"How did you know?" he asked, and for the first time there was an uncertainty in his voice, an intimation of doubt. "How did you find this one, precise spot?"

"It was shown to us," she said, and somehow she kept her voice steady, "and it will be shown to others in the future."

"Shown? By whom?" Now the voice was sharp, demanding, yet the touch of fear remained in his eyes. Out of the corner of her eye Sorina could see Merrill inching farther to one side, closer to Amers.

"By Clarice," she said, not knowing if she told the truth or if she lied. "You, if anyone, should know that. You saw her. You saw her spirit. You saw that it recognized you."

And she wondered as she spoke: It sounds so logical; could it be that I *am* telling the truth?

For several seconds Amers' face seemed frozen, his lips parted a fraction of an inch, his eyes riveted on Sorina.

"Yes," he whispered, the sound drawn out like air from a punctured balloon. "I saw it. I saw it . . ."

Another movement, and another, Merrill continued to inch to one side. Soon, Sorina thought, he would be in a position to—

Amers' eyes seemed to focus again, to move toward Merrill, and the gun—

"William Barlow," she said, forcing the words out, and when Amers' eyes snapped back toward her, she rushed on: "William Barlow is buried here. He really *was* kidnaped, wasn't he? Just as some people suspected, just as you yourself said. But he wasn't kidnaped by the brothers of the man he killed, was he? And he wasn't hired or kidnaped by Merrill, either. He was kidnaped by you. And he was killed by you. And then buried here, so that everyone would think that he had escaped after killing Abel and his family."

Forcing herself not to shift her eyes so much as a fraction of a degree toward Merrill, tensing herself to plunge out of the way when Merrill made his move, she went on:

"And tonight? What happened tonight? Did you plan for it to look as if one of them had tried to burn the house down, to conceal evidence, and been caught at it? They fought and knocked each other out? Or did you have something better, more clever? Something as clever as the kidnaping and murder of William Barlow?"

Again Amers seemed to return from some distant retreat and take up residence in the body that stood facing them, leveling a gun at them.

"As I said, you left me no choice. You and Barlow—and Clarice. You left me no choice, just as you leave me none now." As he spoke, some of the tension seemed to be easing out of his voice, and Sorina wondered:

How many more minutes—or seconds—do we have? Is this how it was when Clarice had died? Is this how it felt? Would Merrill have time to—

"Howald!" Amers' voice spit out the name, and his gun shifted abruptly to center on Merrill—yet he didn't fire. He only motioned for Merrill to move back to Sorina's side.

"Are you going to kill us while all these people are here?" Merrill asked. "Do you think you can get away with it? There are a dozen firemen and half as many police less than two hundred yards away."

"What alternative do you offer? I can't possibly let you go, not now."

"Yes, you can," Sorina said, and again she was surprised at the steadiness of her voice. "You need help, Norris. You must realize that, or you—"

His face twisted as she spoke, and she knew instantly that she had said the wrong thing.

"You *are* one of them! I needn't have worried about you, not at all! You're just like them!"

She could see his finger tightening on the trigger, and, uselessly, she moved her hands, holding them in front of herself, as if to—

Suddenly, from the darkness surrounding their island of light, a screaming, hissing missile launched itself through the air, a white and tan and orange mass of fur and claws and teeth. From somewhere behind Amers it came as if shot from a catapult, its eyes—and the carnelian—glittering like three shooting stars.

Amers jerked around, just in time to catch the full fury of the attack in his face. The gun went off harmlessly, the bullets thudding into the ground, and then the gun followed them as he released his hold and clawed at the screeching, hissing demon locked over his face.

Then his own screams blended with those of the cat, and he was staggering backward, both hands clawing blindly, trying to get a grip on the writhing mass. Merrill dashed forward, grabbing the gun from where it had fallen.

Still Amers screamed, somehow unable to grasp the animal and hurl it from him, and as he staggered, Sorina could see spots of red splattering the fur, spattering on Amers' shirt.

For an instant—just an instant—the feeling of duality that she had felt when she had first entered the house came over her again, and she was, in that one frozen moment, both Sorina Stark and a nameless, avenging spirit, spitting and clawing and crying, slashing in a frenzy at the face that had hovered over her at her own simultaneous death and birth.

Then, as suddenly as it had come, it was gone, and at the same instant a flailing ball of white dotted with red sailed through the air and into the darkness.

And it was over.

Amers, his hands clutching at a face that dripped red, fell backwards onto the ground, and the hoarse rasping that grated from his throat gradually subsided until there was only a soft moaning.

Sorina herself felt a clammy coldness on her face and a wrenching at her stomach, then a whirling dizziness as everything began to catch up with her. She felt herself falling.

And as she fell, from somewhere in her whirling mind came the final thought: After what I've been through tonight, it's about time I got some rest.

Then there was blackness.

"I don't suppose you saved any of the tapes?" Mrs. Strickland's words were closer to a statement than a question, and Sorina only shook her head.

Mrs. Strickland sighed. "Somehow I didn't think you had."

She turned toward Merrill Howald, who stood a few feet behind them, also looking up at the now empty shell of West House.

"And I suppose," she went on, "this means that the Society doesn't get the money after all? Or the history? What with the will being a phony, I mean."

Merrill took his eyes from the remains of the house, and what might have been a faint smile appeared through the beard.

"Whatever gave you that idea?" he asked. "I know things didn't work out quite like Jim and I planned, but, in a way, we got what we were looking for. Why should I want the money back?"

Mrs. Strickland hesitated, glancing from Merrill to

Sorina and back. "And the money you were going to pay for the history?"

"That depends on Sorina." He looked toward her as he spoke. "That offer of a job still holds, if you want it. And there's no reason why it couldn't be right here. If you want to spend some of your time collecting—what's the term? oral history?—there's no reason you couldn't. I'm sure we could run a series of articles on local history in the *Journal*. And if Mrs. Strickland wants custody of the tapes you would make during your interviews . . ."

"You're serious? You—" Mrs. Strickland broke off, turned again toward Sorina.

"But you—*would* you be interested in anything like that?"

Sorina thought for a moment. This wasn't the type of history—or the type of writing—she had thought she would be interested in, and yet . . .

Her mind went back to the tapes she had recorded, particularly the ones made by Bessie Platte, with her dozens of stories and memories. And the other people she had been told about but had not had a chance to talk with yet. Lurlie, with no first name that anyone knew, and only one leg, who used to baby-sit for anyone who would bring their children to her tiny shack. Annie Simpson, who had, among other things, sold herbs from door to door and gotten a reputation among the youngsters of the twenties and thirties and even the forties as a witch, but who was really just a nice old lady who now lived with a niece (so they said) and her husband, themselves both in their seventies now.

No, this wasn't quite what she had had in mind when she had minored in history. There was none of the "sweep" or grand scope one normally associated with history, but this was, she suspected, more interesting and, in a way, more rewarding. And, of course, there was Merrill . . .

"Yes," she said finally, "I think I would be. Provided, of course—"

She turned to look pointedly at the mashed fender and warped bumper and wheel of her station wagon, which still stood back among the trees where she had maneuvered it the night before. "Provided I have something to get around to all the interviews in."

"Don't worry," Merrill said, "I'm getting you a new one, whether you stay or not. It's a damned small payment for still being alive."

Sorina was silent for a moment, then grinned. "If you think I'm going to turn it down, you're crazy. But don't expect me to do the same thing again. I only break down the door of a burning building once for a man. After that, it's up to him."

He laughed as he took one of her hands in his, but there was a grim undertone to the sound. "With Norris safely tucked away for the foreseeable future, once should be enough."

"I sincerely hope so," Sorina said, a touch of seriousness in her voice too. "Next time there might not be a—"

She felt something brush against her ankle. Her eyes darted downward, and as she saw what was there, rubbing cozily back and forth against her leg, she stiffened, her hand tightening on Merrill's.

"—a cat to wake me up in time . . ." she finished her sentence in a whisper.

She reached down slowly and picked up the cat. It was mostly white, with patches of tan and orange, the hair long and silky, and its eyes—

A small sigh of relief escaped her lips as she saw that the eyes were a deep green, not the eerie brownish red that she had half feared.

And there was, of course, no collar, and the animal was purring loudly.

As if—the thought jolted through Sorina sharply, and she felt a momentary chill of disorientation—as if it were now free to be itself once again, to return, somehow, from a shadow world to the real world, where cats were only cats and did not awaken people from a sound sleep just in time to save their lives—where spirits did not exist except in the minds of the beholders.

Gently she set it back on the ground. "Come on, cat, do you need a home now?"

As if in answer, it again began rubbing back and forth against her legs and, as the three of them started slowly back to Merrill's car, it sat for a moment, watching their retreating backs, and then, with an almost inaudible mewing, trotted after them.